DISORDER AND SERFDOM

J P GADSTON

MIND UTOPIA PRESS

DISORDER AND SERFDOM
© J P Gadston 2019
Cover Art by Sarah Anderson
Editing by Michelle Dunbar Editing Services

All rights reserved. No part of this publication may be reproduced, distributed, or transmitted in any form or by any means, including photocopying, scanning, uploading to the internet, recording, or other electronic or mechanical methods, without the prior written permission of the publisher and/or author, except in the case of brief quotations for reviews.

This is a work of fiction. Names, characters, businesses, places, events, and incidents are either the products of the author's imagination, or used in a fictitious manner. Any resemblance to persons, living or dead, or actual events is entirely coincidental.

First published in 2019 by Mind Utopia Press

ISBN NUMBER: 9781076879813

*For those of you in a dark place,
may you find the path to self-salvation.*

PROLOGUE

Marcus Smith shook his head. In his thirty years as a holographic technician at the University of Oxford, he had never once lost a student to virtual-reality. The program was supposed to give the students an insight into the era they were studying – not trap them there.

William Thompson tapped a screen on his console. 'He's showing some unusual brain activity.'

'I can see that,' he snapped. 'You ran all the tests before you put him under?'

Thompson nodded.

'No unusual results?'

'I don't think so.'

'You don't *think* so?' He nudged Thompson aside and scrolled through Joel Benson's pre-immersion assessment results. Nothing obvious stood out. Joel had entered the twenty-first century smoothly, assimilated into a historical figure of his choice, and as far as he could tell, all the safety procedures had been adhered to. And yet Joel resisted all attempts to pull him out of the program.

'So, how do we get him back?'

SERFDOM AND DISORDER

Marcus looked across the room to where Joel lay inside one of the isolation pods. 'We need to know exactly where he is in the program – and when – and whose identity he's taken. We could try inserting some access points to get inside and get his attention, remind him who he is and hopefully, he'll come back to us.'

'And if he doesn't?'

Marcus chewed on his bottom lip. If Joel was as deeply immersed as Marcus feared, there was every chance he would remain in the program, never realising that his real life was in the twenty-third century.

1

It was supposed to be a pleasant night out in the Libra Arms pub with his girlfriend, Veronica Jones. Unfortunately, pleasantness and a good night out had become a dewy-eyed fantasy. Tony Harrison wiped his sweaty palms on the faux leather sofa, cringing as a raspy voice rose from the table behind him. Plaistow's plastic gangsters – a bunch of old has-beens – were comparing notes on men they'd beaten up in their youth, with each orator sounding more desperate to impress than the last. They spewed stories about their criminal past and how many villains they'd mixed with. Tony rolled his eyes. It was complete bollocks and bravado.

Tony looked around, observing the confident, street-hardened geezers looking for trouble. They glared about the pub, looking for a fight. Other men engaged in crude, booze-fuelled talk; barmaids responded in kind. At the furthermost edge of the bar, a drunk pissed himself as he tumbled to the floor. Two useless-looking herberts laughed and then jumped back as the contents of the drunk's guts projected forward. The younger of the two thudded his fist on the bar to get attention.

SERFDOM AND DISORDER

'Someone get this fucker out!'

Saturday night was always the same in the Libra: alive with criminals, construction workers, and football hooligans. The smell of cheap shower gel, deodorant, aftershave, and perfume irritated Tony's throat. The pub's DJ added his own blend of tackiness, sporting an open-necked black shirt and a gold-coloured medallion. He played a disco song from the eighties. Every time the chorus came on, he pulled down the faders on the mixing deck. The men raised their pint glasses and replaced the lyrics with 'suck my helmet' in a tuneless sing-along. Their wives and girlfriends stood around chatting, oblivious of their partners' brain-dead bravado.

Tony gritted his teeth. He couldn't endure another second. He rubbed the back of his neck and stared at the beige wallpaper in front of him. A weird feeling swept over him, oddness hitting him like a hammer. He couldn't describe the sensation, and it took him a moment to snap out of the self-induced trance. He stared into his watered-down beer, blinking hard. 'Dingy shithole,' he muttered.

Veronica's silence said it all. She looked as pissed off as he felt.

Tony struggled to his feet, putting his weight on the arm of the sofa. The room lurched, and he lost his balance, stumbling into the table and chairs occupied by the plastic gangsters. Empty glasses fell to the dirty-grey vinyl flooring, and a figure rose in front of him but blurred into the background. The sudden urge to get outside overwhelmed him.

He pushed through the booze-infused vocalists,

headed towards the nearest exit. An arm slipped through his, and Veronica's voice shrilled through the noise, 'Is everything okay?'

Tony didn't respond. His legs wobbled, and sweat poured down his forehead. He shoved the door open and stumbled into the smoking area – a walled-off concrete square littered with fag butts, urine-sprinkled walls, and a padlocked gate.

The bitter January air whipped his face, bringing him back into focus. Veronica flicked her long black hair over her shoulder. 'Are you sure you're okay?'

Tony nodded. 'Yeah, I think so.'

'I thought...' She drew her teeth over her bottom lip. 'Well, you looked so bored in there I was wondering if...' She sighed. 'Tony, do you still like me? Because if you want to – '

'I like you more than you'll ever know.' Tony caressed Veronica's hair. 'I don't feel so good.' It wasn't a complete lie. He wasn't ready to tell Veronica everything about himself just yet. They'd only been dating a few months, but she was the best thing that had ever happened to him. The truth was, he was sick of hanging around dives like the Libra, pretending to be somebody he wasn't. He wanted to move away but couldn't afford it.

She wrapped her arms around him and squeezed close, tilting her face towards his. She smiled and then laughed gently. Tony's lips met hers, and she closed her eyes, trembling beneath his touch. They were the only ones foolish enough to be out in the smoking area in sub-zero temperatures, which was ironic as neither of them smoked.

SERFDOM AND DISORDER

Veronica pulled away with a smile. 'Maybe we should go somewhere else?'

Tony nodded and put his hand on the small of her back as he ushered her towards the door. A stream of profanity seared the silence, followed by glass shattering. Veronica hesitated.

'This is one of the better dives around these parts, you know.' He smiled. 'Look, we'll finish our drink and —'

The door crashed open, and two middle-aged men tumbled outside. Tony recognised the thick-set man in the black leather bomber jacket in an instant: Shaun Murphy. Tony grabbed hold of Veronica, but with no space to step around the warring duo, they backed against the wall, unwilling spectators to the mindless violence.

Shaun Murphy wasn't a man to mess around with. He held the other man's head in a tight lock and aimed a series of punches at his face. Blood spurted from his victim's nose, and when he broke free from the clinch, another landed on the point of his chin. His legs wobbled as more blows landed on his face. An uppercut caught his jaw, producing a sickening bone-crunching sound, and he crumpled to the floor in a heap.

Veronica buried her face in Tony's back, her breathing erratic and out of rhythm. Tony wanted to shut his eyes, but morbid curiosity took over. Murphy lined himself up, drew back his leg as if taking a penalty, then kicked his victim in the mouth. A horrid crunch broke the silence; blood pooled on the frozen ground, broken teeth too.

Veronica clung tighter to Tony. 'Is he dead?'

Tony shook his head. The unconscious man's chest still moved up and down.

Murphy used his hand to adjust his messed-up hair, which was cropped short at the sides and only a little longer on the top. He straightened his jacket and the thick gold chain around his neck, then leaned over the other man and spat in his face.

Tony stiffened, sickened by Murphy's casual response to dishing out a beating. Behind him, Veronica's sobs were hysterical. She buried her face deeper in his back as if it were a shield protecting her from the evil she had just witnessed.

Murphy stepped forward. His six-feet-two height put him some inches above Tony. 'Tell that woman of yours to keep her fucking mouth shut, or I'll slice her open.' To make his point clear, he pulled a cut-throat razor from inside his jacket pocket.

Dread flooded every organ in Tony's body. He put his arm around Veronica's shoulder and held her head to his chest, desperate to usher her away. However, Murphy wasn't done. He bent over the unconscious man, hauled him up, and threw him into a corner. The man crashed against tables and chairs, falling to the floor like a rag doll.

The path back to the pub was clear, and as Murphy approached his half-dead target, Tony and Veronica scurried into the pub. They weaved their way through the crowd, grabbed their coats, and headed to the main door, taking the street that ran parallel to the pub.

Veronica couldn't speak. She had a shaken, terrified look in her eyes, and she seemed to have lost all the colour from her face.

SERFDOM AND DISORDER

Tony's heart beat furiously. Worry turned his stomach and toyed with his mind. He wanted Veronica to know how dangerous Shaun Murphy was and how serious his threat was, but she was in no position to hear it just yet.

'Where are we going?' she asked with a shaky breath.

'My place. It's more civilised there.'

As they walked through the cold, dark streets to his flat, Tony's mind spun. He kept looking over his shoulder, half expecting to see Murphy trailing behind. He battled with his decision to tell Veronica about Murphy. He was a big player around Plaistow, the top man in the No Mercy firm, and he had his fingers in a lot of rackets. Drugs, prostitutes, firearms… Anyone who crossed swords with Murphy ended up dead in a gutter.

Better to put her on guard.

He wrapped his arm around her shoulder and pulled her a little closer. 'Veronica, there's something I have to tell you. That man who carried out the assault…'

The rest of the sentence died on his lips. How was he supposed to say what he needed to say without freaking her out or driving her away from him? She was shivering beneath his touch – from shock, or the cold – perhaps both, but he couldn't *not* tell her. She had a right to know what they were up against.

Veronica shrugged his arm off her shoulder and stepped back.

'His name's Shaun Murphy, and… well… he's not the sort of man we want to mess with.'

'So we're in this mess because we were standing outside a pub minding our own business?'

'Just… don't talk about it – to anybody. Okay?'

She wrapped her arms around her body with a shiver.

'Everything will be fine.'

That was bullshit, of course, but he hoped it would reassure her. He prayed the man would pull through. It would make things a lot less complicated.

2

Rawstone Walk, the dark, dank-looking council estate where Tony had the misfortune to live, loomed into view. Brown and black brickwork surrounded them as they walked through a maze of houses, flats, and two-storey maisonettes, all crammed together into a big heap. It resembled a prison block, a testament to how the higher reaches of society viewed people like Tony.

His nose twitched as they approached the stairwell to his block. The sickly-sweet scent of skunk weed drifted towards them, and as they drew closer, thick white smoke floated out.

A gang of red-eyed youths, aged about sixteen or seventeen, lounged on the dimly lit stairwell. Their childish giggles confirmed they were stoned out of their heads. Tony's stomach lurched. Some poor bloke had had the fuck beaten out of him the week before last. He hoped this lot weren't responsible.

One of the boys glanced up, giving him a toothy grin. 'Well, look what we've got here, a loved-up couple. Tell you what, why don't you go indoors and leave your woman with us? We'll give her a good seeing to.'

Veronica clung tighter to Tony as their laughter echoed around the stairwell.

'Come on, lads.' He wanted to punch them in the face, teach them a lesson, but decided on the softly-softly approach instead. He didn't want to stress Veronica out anymore, not tonight.

As the seconds ticked by, the throbbing in his head intensified, but instead of a stand-off, the boys put their backs against the wall and made space for Tony and Veronica to pass. He didn't question their motives, as strange as it was. He grabbed Veronica's hand and led her through the stench of skunk weed smoke. Some of the boys glared at Tony; others made sexual gestures to Veronica, sticking their tongues out. Tony held his breath until they reached the top of the stairs.

'Count your lucky stars this gear is making us feel so good,' one of the youths shouted after them.

Tony ignored them. He hurried Veronica along the balcony and when he reached his flat, forced his key into the lock, turned it, and shoulder-charged the door. He stormed into the hallway. Veronica wrapped her arms around him. 'Let's turn on the TV and relax with a few drinks, shall we?'

She disappeared into the kitchen while Tony went through to the living room. He lay on the brown leather sofa with his legs stretched out, switching on the TV with the remote, and then flicking through the channels before settling for an old sci-fi program. A character teleported out of a dangerous situation. Tony sighed. He wished he could teleport out of the shithole of an estate he called home.

Veronica came through with the drinks, minus her

warm jacket. Her style of dress wasn't too classy, as they'd only gone to the Libra Arms. A crew neck jumper, dark blue jeans, and knee-high leather boots. It suited her, and her face was made up nice, too, favouring natural-looking makeup. She handed Tony a can of Belgium lager. He sat upright, and she settled down beside him, sipping a vodka ice.

Tony took a sip of beer, and his vision distorted and blurred almost instantaneously. He gripped the arm of the sofa as the walls closed in around him. A bright, luminous light stung his eyes as he moved towards it, but in a matter of seconds, the sensation passed.

What the hell...?

He blinked, breathing hard. Could a few mouthfuls of skunk weed cause hallucinations? No. He glanced at Veronica, wondering if she had experienced it, but she seemed engrossed with the TV. He caressed her hair, and she cuddled in closer.

The doorbell cut the silence in two, followed by urgent hammering on the door. Icy dread shivered down his spine – it was eleven-thirty at night.

'It's probably those idiots from the stairs,' Veronica said.

Tony forced a smile. 'I'd gamble it's a pizza delivery sent to the wrong address. Happens all the time.'

'I hope you're right.'

Tony groaned as he eased himself out of his comfortable chair. He approached the door and, for the briefest of moments, debated on whether to open it. He even thought about getting a knife from the kitchen but decided against it.

When he opened it, he froze. It was Pete Foster, one

of Shaun Murphy's 'heavies' from the No Mercy firm, and he looked every bit the gangster. His black hair was slicked back, and he wore a navy-blue knee-length woollen coat, V-shaped at the top that revealed a white shirt, a blue silk tie, and dark trousers. His face and brown eyes were icy cold, but his looks weren't as menacing as the cosh he was carrying. 'I understand you witnessed a skirmish outside the Libra Arms?'

Tony shook his head. 'Not me, mate. Didn't see a thing.'

'Make sure that remains the case. If I find out you've been shooting your mouth off ...' Foster's gaze lingered on him. 'How's your Uncle Charlie doing, by the way? Keeping well, I hope.'

'Y-yes. Thank you.'

Foster backed away, a smug grin on his face. Tony shut the door and leaned his forehead against it, struggling to find his composure. He understood the threat, and if they had information about his Uncle Charlie, they might even know about Veronica's family. Murphy made it his business to know things.

Tony took a deep breath and headed back to the living room.

Veronica looked up. 'Who was it?'

'Some bloke trying to sell a watch.'

'At this time of night?'

Tony shrugged. 'Junkie, probably.' He tucked a loose lock of Veronica's hair behind her ear and settled down beside her. 'Nothing for us to worry about.'

He leaned towards her, pressing his lips to hers, but his heart wasn't in it and he pulled away.

Veronica frowned. 'Are you all right, Tony?'

SERFDOM AND DISORDER

'I'm fine.'

'I still get the impression you don't like me as much as you say you do.'

Tony stood up, pulling Veronica with him. He forced Murphy, Foster, and the No Mercy firm to the back of his mind and kissed her with renewed passion. He slipped a hand inside the waistband of her jeans and unbuttoned them, then ushered her towards the bedroom.

They reached the heights of ecstasy together. Tony's brain ached like it had split in two. The strange sensation of the walls closing in on him returned. The bedroom disappeared, and a tunnel of luminous light materialised, dragging him towards it.

He squeezed his eyes shut, willing himself back into the bedroom. He envisaged Veronica's naked body beside him: the smell of her perfume, the feel of her body, her smile, her touch.

'Tony? Tony, please tell me what's wrong?'

His eyes snapped open. Veronica's beautiful green eyes stared down at him, concern etching her face.

'You know you can talk to me, don't you? It doesn't matter what it is, I – '

He put a finger over her lips. 'I'm fine. Really. It's been a long week. I'm just… tired.'

Veronica gave off an impatient huff. 'Well, whatever it is, I'm here for you, and I'm a good listener.'

He kissed her lips. 'I don't know what I'd do without you.'

3

Rawstone Walk was a tranquil place on a Sunday morning. All the chaos that went on in the week came to a temporary standstill. Besides the occasional overground train going by, it was the epitome of peace and quiet.

Tony pried his eyes open. They were dry and full of grit – not the best thing to encounter when trying to wake in the morning. He rubbed them then looked around, determined to find out where that godforsaken chime was coming from. He didn't know why he'd set the alarm for a Sunday morning, but his first attempt to lunge for it failed. He tried again and managed to whack the clock from the bedside table to the floor. It landed with a thud, but the ding continued. Tony inched forward, crawling over the mass beside him. He reached for the clock, regretting his decision in an instant. The pulse in his head intensified, and he didn't bother fumbling with the buttons. He grabbed the alarm clock and lobbed it towards the wall – *that* shut it up.

Sheer grit got him back on the horizontal. He lay beside Veronica, breathing hard and wondering when

SERFDOM AND DISORDER

he'd become more responsible. He'd had enough of drinking but found it difficult, come the weekend, not to have a drink. After working all week in a job he hated and the pressure of living in an area he felt trapped in, drinking offered him some solace, a fool's paradise.

Veronica hadn't stirred. She lay beside him like a frozen beauty in a deep trance. Everything about her was enticing. Her laugh, her smile, every rhythmic breath. She had done something to him he couldn't explain. Being close to her made him feel... whole.

As much as Tony hated the idea, he had to get up, though getting to his feet wasn't one of his better ideas. The room lurched, and he fell backwards, missing the soft landing the bed would have afforded him and crashed to the floor. He groaned and staggered to his feet, then headed in the general direction of the kitchen. His throat was as dry as a parchment of leather.

Sunlight reflected off the white tiles, and he squeezed his eyes shut as his hand brushed along the worktop towards the kettle.

Turning his back on the light, he glanced in the mirror and winced at the gaunt-looking face staring back at him. His unshaven face made him look like an extra from a spaghetti western. His hair looked as if someone had poured oil all over it, and he had heavy bags under the eyes.

Tony tipped the steaming hot water into a cup and added a dash of milk. Most of it spilled over the side. He didn't care. The sight of the teabag stewing in water made him froth at the mouth. Once it was stewed to perfection, he took a long slurp from the cup.

His brain came around at a snail's pace. He stared

into the teacup, pondering what had happened outside the Libra. Violence was an everyday reality around these parts, but watching a man get beaten half to death, bringing trouble to his doorstep, that was something else. And what the hell was that freaky vision about?

Never mind the vision. Shaun Murphy was the problem here. If that man died, they would be witnesses to a murder. Veronica didn't deserve to get dragged into that shit – and neither did he.

He refilled the kettle, slammed it into the base, and tossed the teaspoon into the sink. He tried to stop the negative thoughts, but whatever way he looked at it, the outlook wasn't good. The hangover wasn't helping either.

Veronica sauntered into the kitchen, her face as pale as Tony's, her movements slow and cumbersome. She seemed to have trouble keeping her eyes open too. She poured herself a cup of tea and joined Tony at the breakfast table.

'I take it you'll be going to see your Uncle Charlie this morning?'

'Yeah, once I finish my tea and make myself decent.'

His uncle lived a short distance away. Like Tony, Charlie Harrison had academic leanings, but unlike his nephew, had engaged in a life of crime. His involvement with a gang of armed robbers in his early thirties had resulted in him being arrested for a bank job in central London. The twenty-year prison sentence was a massive wake-up call, forcing him to take a look at his life. He shunned the villains and turned to books, spending all his time in prison studying. His fellow cons mocked and vilified him, but after a lot of determination and hard work, Charlie completed his A-levels and had received an honours degree in criminal psychology and a Master's in the same subject.

Charlie came out of prison after serving twelve demanding years. He was in his early seventies now and had long-since turned his back on the criminal fraternity. He chose to live a quiet life with his wife, Doris, but still had contacts with the villains from his past, if the need arose.

'Did you want to come? Uncle Charlie would love to see you again.'

Veronica smiled but shook her head. 'I have some studying to do, if that's okay with you?'

'Of course it is.'

Tony had nothing but admiration for Veronica. She had a great job in one of the top banks in the city and a degree in psychology, but she was constantly pushing herself to achieve more. The promotion she was going for would open a lot of doors.

'You'll be running that bank one of these days.'

She grinned. 'That's the plan.'

He laughed. 'You're amazing, d'you know that?'

It was hard to believe they were from the same area, though she had grown up on one of the nicer estates and gone to a better school than he had. Tony had done okay, passing most of his exams, but his dad had dismissed the idea of further education. Ten years on, he was still dreaming about bettering himself. Uncle Charlie had convinced him to sign up for a vocational course at the local adult education college, but as much as he liked the idea of returning to education, he wasn't entirely sure he was cut out for it.

He sighed and stood, feeling a hell of a lot better for having a cup of tea, almost human in fact. 'I won't be long anyway.'

'Don't rush on my account. I've got plenty to keep me busy.'

The dreary weather was no better than the night before. It was grey skies and icy walkways all round, and there wasn't a soul in sight as Tony crossed the railway bridge. It stank of piss, and there was dog shit and empty beer cans everywhere. That was the problem with Rawstone Walk – no one gave a damn about it. The council came in now and again to clear the rubbish away or paint over the graffiti, but within days, it was back to looking like a rubbish dump.

He snapped out of his mood upon reaching Charlie's door. Tony always felt semi-excited at seeing his favourite uncle, and he hit the street door's brass knocker with enthusiasm. The door opened and there stood Charlie, about six feet tall with thinning, grey hair in a side-parting and wearing steel-rimmed glasses. Dressed in a cardigan, trousers, and slippers.

'Tony, my son. Come in, come in.'

He was greeted by the aroma of fresh, homemade, traditional English cooking. It seemed to blend with the flowered wallpaper and patterned burgundy carpet. With Charlie's passion for reading, there were a few bookcases crammed with a variety of tomes around the living room. He sported a grin as he sat on Charlie's burgundy velvet sofa. 'I hope Doris will save some of that food for me.'

'You could do with some of her treacle pudding and

SERFDOM AND DISORDER

custard – fatten you up a bit.'

Tony patted his lean stomach. 'Yeah.'

Charlie sat in his reclining armchair. He looked at home, cosy. Everything about Uncle Charlie's house felt welcoming. Tony loved looking around the place, at the books on the shelf, the pictures on the wall, ornaments on the wooden shelves.

'Do you want a cup of tea?'

'No thanks, Uncle Charlie, I've just had one.'

Charlie was more like a dad than his real one had been. He was always telling him not to cave into peer pressure and fall into the same traps he had. Growing up, Tony had managed to keep out of any serious trouble. He hoped to make some new friends when he started college. He was tired of trying to fit into the usual mindset around these parts. He wanted to be himself and have friends who liked him for who he was. Only his Uncle Charlie, Aunt Doris, and Veronica knew about his aspirations. His so-called mates would have laughed at the idea of him returning to education.

'You all right there, Tony? You look a bit lost in thought.'

Tony nodded. 'I'm fine. I was just thinking about college.'

'Second thoughts?'

'Nerves.'

'You'll be fine. You might not think it, but you've got the brains to go all the way, if you want. You'll regret it if you don't.'

'No, I want to do it.'

'But?'

Tony shrugged.

'It would fill me with pride to see you do well.'

'I'll try.'

Charlie smiled. 'So… what's *really* bothering you?'

That was *so* Uncle Charlie. Nothing slipped his notice.

'I… er… I had an edgy moment last night.'

'Oh?'

Tony shook his head and placed the palm of his hand over his face. Charlie frowned and levered himself out of his armchair. He crept towards the living room door, shutting it. 'Whatever it is, Tony, it won't leave these four walls. You of all people should know that.'

He returned to his seat and listened as Tony told Charlie about the fight at the Libra Arms. 'And then I had a knock on my door from one of Murphy's henchmen, Pete Foster. He threatened me, and he made sure I saw the cosh he was carrying too.'

Charlie didn't seem surprised. 'Keep a low profile; it'll blow over in a few weeks.' He glanced at the clock on the mantelpiece, grabbed his TV remote from the coffee table, and pointed it at the television in the corner of the room. 'Local news should be on about now.'

Tony, together with Charlie, had a hunger for news, local news more so. Every Sunday, when Tony called round, watching the news together became a weekly ritual. They watched the national news first, with the stiff-necked newsreader droning on about rising crime rates and the lack of police officers on the streets to deal with it. After five minutes of adverts and a preview of a new drama starting that night, the local news blared out.

'A man was savagely attacked outside the Libra Arms

pub last night. The victim is in critical condition at Newham General Hospital. The police are asking witnesses to contact them with information. You can contact them in confidence on this number...'

Tony's eyes widened. He wrung his hands together and wiped his sweaty palms on his trousers.

Charlie turned off the TV. 'Aren't you heading up to Sheffield to work on the railways this week? Maybe you should take Veronica with you. All this fuss will have blown over by the time you get back. It's two weeks you're away for, isn't it?

'Depends on the state of the track.'

'Take her anyway.'

Tony wasn't sure Veronica would appreciate being stuck in a strange city for two weeks, more so when he would be out working on the railway all day.

'I'll ask her.'

Charlie smiled. 'She's an intelligent woman. She'll go.'

He nodded but didn't share Charlie's confidence. Tony couldn't see her putting her employment at risk for the sake of a pub brawl.

Charlie leaned forward. 'If things get heavy around here, I'll put the feelers out for you.'

'It'll be fine.' Tony forced a smile. He regretted opening his mouth now. Uncle Charlie was a pensioner. He didn't need any involvement in this. He might have been tough in his youth, but he was no match for Murphy's heavies, regardless of the contacts he had. Besides, Tony had been bought up to fight his own battles. The last thing he wanted was for anyone to think he was weak.

'I'd better get moving, Uncle Charlie.' He rose to his feet. 'Sorry to drag you into all this.'

'You've got nothing to be sorry about. Murphy and his firm have every idea about my background. They won't try anything. Now get, before I boot you out the door.'

They shook hands and hugged each other. Tony's thoughts drifted to Veronica. As soon as he stepped out of the house, he pulled his phone out of his pocket and called her. His breathing quickened as he waited for her to answer, imagining the worst. When she answered, his words blurted out in a rush. 'I'm on my way back, Veronica. Don't open the door to anyone.'

'What do you mean?'

'Just do as I say. I'll be home in a few minutes.'

Tony quickened his pace. The ice crunched under his feet as he stomped towards his flat. The cold air gave him a renewed sense of alertness, clearing his head.

Out the corner of his eye, Tony noticed a navy-blue 7-series BMW crawling along the road, matching his pace. He kept his eyes on the path ahead. He didn't want the occupants to know he'd seen them. Better to act normal, or as normal as he could manage in the circumstances. He stepped onto the piss-stenched bridge, and a golden light filled his vision, blinding him for a moment. He propped himself against the barrier, leaning his weight against it as he tried to draw breath. Ice no longer crunched beneath his feet, and the stench of rancid piss disappeared. He heard a voice, like an echo, but so distant that the words were too faint to make out.

When he blinked, he wasn't on the bridge but

outside his block of flats, as grim and grey in daylight as they were at night. Some boys stood a few feet away, pointing and giggling at him. Tony let go of the wall he was hugging and stepped towards them. The boys turned and ran, laughing. Tony staggered to a halt, holding a hand to his head as he tried to make sense of what had just happened.

He must have blacked out, but that didn't explain how he'd got from the bridge to the flats, or why he was clinging to the wall. The BMW had gone, though.

Tony fumbled in his jean pockets for his door key and hurried up the staircase to his flat. His hands were shaking so much he found it difficult to get his key in the lock.

When he finally got the door open, he rushed inside, slamming the door behind him. The whole flat shuddered. 'Veronica!' he called as he rushed forward. 'Are you okay?'

Veronica looked up from her book. She had rearranged all the cushions and looked quite at home. 'Tony, what – ?'

'We're heading north.'

'We?'

'That bloke's in a critical condition.'

Her eyes widened. 'How do you know?'

'It's headline news.'

Veronica's mouth froze open. She dropped her book and ran from the room. Tony winced at the gagging noises coming from the bathroom. She wouldn't be in this mess if it wasn't for him. What the hell did she see in him, anyway?

When she emerged, her face was pasty and she held

her arms around her chest. 'I'll...' She paused. 'I'll let my work know, but I think... I have holidays I can take.'

Tony put an arm around Veronica. 'We'll be fine. We just need to keep our heads down for a while. The fuss will pass. You'll see.'

He packed for Sheffield in rapid time, and they hurried towards Veronica's gleaming white Audi TT Coupe. Tony scanned the car park, always alert for potential trouble coming his way. Seeing nothing untoward, he dumped his bags in the boot and jumped in the passenger side.

Veronica turned the key in the ignition as a black Mercedes came around the corner, driving up close to them. She pulled the gear into reverse, and the car screeched backwards. Her hands trembled, and her breathing was short and sharp.

The Audi spun around and jerked to a halt, just missing a collision with the Mercedes. Tears streamed down Veronica's face. She scrubbed her face with the sleeves of her jacket as the Mercedes reversed into a parking space.

'We need to relax,' Tony said.

'Relax!'

Tony winced. 'Being upset just makes everything worse. You can pull through this. You're a tough lady.'

Veronica wiped the tears from her face. She took a long breath and nodded. Tony sighed as they left Rawstone Walk behind them.

4

Tony and Veronica spent an uneventful couple of weeks in Sheffield. He wished he could have stayed longer, but the job ended and he had no choice but to return to the shithole he called home. He spent the first couple of nights scouring social media and news sites for updates on the incident, but besides the initial write-up, there was nothing to read.

Veronica had planned a night out with her friends, while Tony had been coerced into a night down The Coach with his friends. He'd have preferred to spend a quiet night indoors with a movie or book and a few beers, but it was one of the lad's birthday's, so he could hardly say no.

The Coach and Horses was a few hundred years old. With its low ceilings, white walls, and black oak panelling, it took anyone who visited back to another time – at least until their senses were overcome with the house music-obsessed DJ. The pub was far too small for that level of noise, but most of the patrons were either too drunk or too high to notice, sometimes both.

Punters trickled out of the toilets, men and women, sniffing loudly and with wide bulging eyes; there was no hiding what they had been up to and they didn't try. It was as if making a display of it made them respectable and streetwise for being drug addicts.

Tony sat at one of the corner tables, surrounded by people he had grown up with but didn't regard as real friends. He quickened his drinking speed, hating the claustrophobic feeling that swept over him. That he had to endure the conversation on the table made matters worse.

'Yeah, we kicked the fuck out of them, didn't we? You remember when we tried to gate-crash that party? Must have been about five years ago now. What a fucking night that was!' Joe Buckton said. His top lip curled, and his narrow eyes flashed with bravado.

Billy Longsmith howled with laughter. 'Yeah, I battered the shit out of that bloke trying to stop us getting in, fucking idiot!'

Tony gripped his glass as he felt his body temperature rise. He had heard that story so many times – they all had – yet they still droned on about it. Joe and Billy were, unfortunately, work colleagues. Of his other four friends, Craig had never worked a day in his life but could somehow afford to drink nearly every night. Ben and Lee worked in construction, and Colin was involved in some petty crime Tony didn't care to know about.

Every one of them looked brain-dead. Their version of reality revolved around violence, crime, and talking about football. In their world, it was all that life offered. Tony couldn't wait to get on the path to academia, broaden his mind, and get away from the bay of pigs engulfing him.

'What's the matter with you then, Tony? You ain't saying much, are you? What's with the depressed look? It's that woman you're seeing, ain't it? You're falling in love with her,' teased Joe. 'He's got it bad, lads. I heard he took her up to Sheffield with him.'

Everyone laughed. As they sniggered, they dipped their fingers in the lager puddles on the table and flicked beer at Tony. Women, to them, were there to have sex with and nothing else.

'That's right, Joe, I'm in love. Bet you don't know what that is.'

'What do you mean?'

The temples at the side of his head pulsated. Tony's hands tightened into fists under the table. Joe was dangerously close to crossing the line.

'Ah, look, he's gone all quiet again. You know why, don't you? It's his turn to go to the bar.'

Tony gave Joe an empty smile and stood with a slight sway. He pushed through hordes of people to get to the bar, mostly walking sideways, and eventually made it to the front of the bar. He ordered the pints then looked over at his table, shouting for one of them to help get the beers back.

The house music continued to thump, and Tony cringed as the walls seemed to close in on him. He held a clammy palm to his temple and breathed deeply. It was the same sensation he'd felt in the Libra Arms. After semi-stumbling around the packed crowd, Tony navigated to the right table. He wanted to down his pint and go home. Everyone else at the table was arguing. Tony glanced at the ceiling and yearned to be anywhere but here.

Billy pointed at a man moving towards them. 'Look. It's Stephen Downer.'

The blond-haired man staggered forward. Stephen was a couple of years younger than Tony, in his mid-twenties, but his boyish looks made him look like a teenager who couldn't hold his drink. His legs twisted and turned in various directions, but eventually, he made it to their table and leaned heavily on it. 'Any of you bastards know what happened to my dad?'

An uncomfortable silence swept across the table as Stephen stared at each of them in turn.

'I'll tell you what the fuck happened then, shall I? My dad was in the Libra having a quiet drink with my mum. Minding their own business. Some scumbag called Shaun Murphy comes in and says something nasty to my mum. She's never even met the man before.'

Stephen swayed around their table. He raised his hand, pointing his finger and ranting at the top of his voice.

Tony bowed his head, unable to look Stephen in the eye. The memory of that evening came back to him, and when he closed his eyes, he saw Murphy kicking and punching the man, even when the victim had fallen unconscious.

Stephen's eyes welled up. 'That piece of shit Murphy… I'll kill him.'

Billy Longsmith jumped up. He grabbed Stephen's arm and shoved him away from their table. No one insulted Shaun Murphy in public. It was a death sentence if anyone from the No Mercy firm overheard.

'I will sort that fucker out, and *no one's* going to stop

SERFDOM AND DISORDER

me!'

Stephen tried to get back to the table, but Billy shoved him back into the crowd. Tony looked away. His eyes widened as he spotted some men from the No Mercy firm entering the pub. Each of them was dressed in a smart suit, shirt, and tie, completely out of place for a night in the Coach and Horses. They glanced around with narrowed eyes, searching the crowd like a pack of dogs at a fox hunt.

Billy pressed his face closer to Stephen's. 'Look, Downer, why don't you disappear? We don't want you here, so piss off!'

Tony got up from his seat and pushed Billy aside. He grabbed Stephen, put his arm around his shoulder, and ushered him through the back door of the pub. 'I feel for you, mate, I really do, but you need to keep your emotions in check.'

Stephen struggled out of Tony's grasp, staggering backwards. 'What would you be like if someone beat *your* dad to a pulp for no reason?'

'You can't mouth off about Sean Murphy like that.'

Tears spilled down Stephen's face as he fell against the wall. 'What if he dies? I can't let this pass. That piece of shit needs sorting out!'

Tony agreed with Stephen, but it was too dangerous to vocalize the fact. He patted Stephen on the shoulder. 'Get yourself a cab and go home. You'll have a clearer head in the morning. If you need someone to talk to, call me.'

He barely knew the man, but the guilt at doing nothing about his dad's assault, saying nothing, was getting the better of him. He took Stephen's phone from him, entered his details, and handed it back. Tony walked him to the cab office around the corner before heading home himself. Flashbacks of the brutal attack overwhelmed him. He wanted to drown his sorrows in the Coach and Horses, but he wasn't going back; not with the No Mercy thugs loitering around. It was better to play it safe and go home, have a few beers, and relax in front of the TV.

As Tony drew close to his flat, his mobile phone rang. It was Joe Buckton. 'What happened to you then? One minute you were outside with Downer, the next you disappeared.'

'That No Mercy firm makes me uneasy. I didn't want to hang around.'

'Yeah, well, we're off to Stratford to have a late drink. You wanna come?'

'Nah, I think I'll pass on that. I'll see you Monday.'

The call ended, and Tony continued on his walk home. A thought came from nowhere – a realization – it was Friday night and the teenagers would be back in his stairwell, smoking dope. He could use the stairwell at the other end of the maisonettes, but that would mean surrendering to the little thugs. If he lost face, his life would be even more miserable.

As Tony continued to walk, an object with a dull shine grabbed his attention – a metal bar about two feet long. He stared at the icy pavement contemplating his next move. If he pulled it out on the mob in the stairwell, it could escalate. They might even be carrying knives… *Fuck it, I've got to defend myself somehow.*

Tony's heartbeat picked up its pace the closer he got. His left hand gripped the cold metal bar, holding it behind his back. Their laughter echoed through the stairwell, and, as was the norm for a Friday night, they sat on the stairs amidst huge plumes of smoke.

'Here he is, boys. Our friend's back.'

The boys glared at Tony through the cannabis-laced mist. A few of them had their hands in their pockets. Tony's heart pumped as if ready to explode. Negotiation wouldn't work, and there was no turning back. Walking away would make matters worse, and besides, his anger was building inside him. He gripped the bar tighter. 'Are you going to let me pass?'

'If you pay us a fee, yeah.'

'Are you having a laugh?'

A knife appeared from one of the youth's pockets, glinting under the stairwell light. Tony pulled the metal bar out from behind his back. 'Come on then, you fucking scum bags. You want a fee? Here's your fucking fee!'

He swung the metal rod at the nearest boy. It cracked against his head, and the boy flopped backwards. The rest of the gang got to their feet and scrambled up the stairs.

Tony's vision blurred as the strange tunnel materialised around him. He heard a voice, softly spoken but distorted. It resembled a half-tuned broadcast from an old radio set. The tunnel disappeared then reappeared, and in-between the back-and-forth sensation, he saw the youth sprawled on the stairwell. Blood had splattered the wall and pooled on the floor. Neighbours poked their heads out of their windows and dogs barked, disturbed by the racket the gang had made as they ran along the upper balcony towards the other stairwell.

The tunnel disappeared and the youths did too, except for the boy slumped in a pool of blood. The overpowering smell of cannabis was still there, and Tony clamped a hand over his nose and mouth as he backed away. He swiped his hand through his hair as he turned and ran, keeping to the recently gritted roads so as not to slip. He chucked the bar into a set of nearby bushes and then got himself as far away from the estate as his legs and lungs would take him.

His hands shook as he rubbed his face. He had nowhere to go. A trip to Uncle Charlie's was out of the question, Veronica would still be out, and his friends would be in Stratford by now. He pulled his coat tighter around his body and kept walking. He imagined the police and ambulance service were at the scene by now, so he couldn't go back just yet.

Everything was going wrong. First, Stephen Downer's dad, and now this. If he had the money he would get as far away from this place as he could and never look back, but he didn't. He was stuck here. Trapped.

Three frozen hours passed before Tony returned to Rawstone Walk. He loitered behind one of cars in the car park, checking to see if he was clear to go back home. The stairs had been taped off by the police and the blood stains were still there, but there wasn't a policeman in sight, which seemed odd.

He wandered to the stairwell at the other end of the block and made his way up the concrete stairs. His movements were laboured, his body frozen. A reassuring thought entered his mind as he approached his street door. None of the neighbours would tell the police what they'd seen. They would be grateful someone had finally sorted the youths out.

He slumped in the armchair in his living room with the central heating turned up as high as it would go, pondering what he had done. Attacking the youth like he had was so out of character for him, and so violent too. He poured himself a Jack Daniels and emptied the bourbon down his throat. A rush of warmth hit his head; he grimaced and poured another. His eyes glazed over, feeling heavy, but his mind kept racing. He couldn't stop thinking about the tunnel with the golden light. The fact he had started seeing it after watching Stephen's dad getting beaten up made him wonder if it was stress related.

Tired and drowsy from too much drink, Tony yawned as his mind battled on. He struggled to keep his eyes open as he staggered from his chair to the bedroom, hoping tomorrow would bring him a hassle-free day.

5

Tony awoke with a head as heavy as an anvil. Thinking Veronica was next to him, he moved his arm across the bed then groaned when he remembered she wasn't there. He lay back instead, raising both arms skyward. *Why, oh why, do I bother boozing?*

His stomach growled as he pictured himself eating a fried bacon sandwich dripping in butter. Then the smell of it entered his mental processing, and saliva dribbled from his mouth. He wiped his mouth with his sleeve cuff. Overwhelmed with hunger, he dragged himself out of bed. He had to have that sandwich.

The events of the previous night weighed heavily on Tony's mind, and the hangover just made it worse. He lumbered to his bedroom window and pulled the net curtain aside. He studied the stairwell entrance where he'd lost his composure, yearning for an ordinary day without any drama or a visit to an odd tunnel with light at the end; although, his biggest concern was a potential visit from the police.

He fried the bacon and then sat in the kitchen, savouring every mouthful of the tasty bacon-and-bread combination. He glanced at the digital radio on the shelf opposite, got up from his chair, and turned it on. Smooth music greeted him. He wondered what it would be like to have sex with Veronica on the kitchen table, he and gulped down his cup of tea, excited about his vision. Some tea went down the wrong way, and he gagged and coughed until his face turned deep red.

A sound startled Tony out of his wishful thinking; his mobile phone vibrated and rang from the kitchen table. He grabbed the phone to see who was calling, but there was no name attached to the number. He sneered as the effort of getting out of his chair became a mountainous task. In what seemed like an eternity, Tony turned off the radio then hesitated, reluctant to answer the call at all. 'Whoever you are, this is not a good time to call.'

'It's me,' a familiar voice said. 'Stephen Downer. We spoke last night.'

Tony's head pounded, dreading what Stephen had to say about his dad's condition.

'Hello? Tony? Are you still there?'

'Sorry, bit of a hangover. Are you okay?'

'Not disturbing you, am I?'

'No, no, you're fine. What's up?'

'I need to get out of this house and stop thinking about my dad. Can we meet up somewhere?'

'Where?'

He scratched his head and did his best not to yawn. They agreed to meet at the Connaught Bridge, opposite the London Regatta Centre in Beckton, at one thirty in the afternoon.

Tony worried about Stephen Downer wanting to

meet him off the beaten track. He had given Stephen his phone number to pacify him, not actually expecting him to call. He tossed the phone on the worktop. His head hurt like he'd received a punch in the skull. He had an eerie feeling about the meeting but couldn't understand why. He turned the radio back on; it helped him think.

His mobile phone rang again, and he jumped. He struggled out of the chair again and recovered the phone. He glanced at the screen, hoping it was anyone other than Stephen Downer. He smiled when he saw Veronica's name.

He wandered out of the kitchen and headed towards the living room. 'Hello, gorgeous, are you coming round later?'

After a little small talk, he broached the subject of Stephen and his dad. 'Would it be possible to give me a lift to Beckton? I've got to meet Stephen and find out what he wants.'

'Yeah, I'll be round in about half an hour.'

He ended the call and returned to the earlier fantasy about Veronica. The more he thought about it, the more he fancied having sex with her on the kitchen table, if she was up for it. His face lit up at the thought of his daydream becoming a reality.

Tony couldn't get rid of the unease in the pit of his stomach as Veronica drove him to Beckton. He rested his hand on his forehead and stared out the window, lost in thought. Veronica glanced at him, and he dropped his arm to his side and forced a smile. 'You know, lots of people on my estate think I'm in a relationship with a drug dealer.'

'What?'

'Yeah, I've overheard a few of my neighbours talking about you and your car. They think you're selling cocaine.'

Veronica stiffened and seemed tongue-tied for a moment. 'Because I have a nice car? How narrow-minded is that? I don't even like parking on the estate in case it gets stolen.'

Tony laughed and tugged at the sleeve on her jacket: 'You bit the bait there, didn't you?'

She rolled her eyes. 'I keep falling for your stupid wind-ups, don't I?'

Tony grinned and kissed her on the cheek. She pulled up beside the bridge, and Tony kissed her again. Her skin felt soft, alluring, and he didn't want to leave her. He shivered as he got out of the car, already hating the Thames-side approach to Connaught Bridge. His heart sank as he waved to Veronica, who pulled away and disappeared into the distance.

He glanced around to see if Stephen Downer had arrived yet. He hadn't, so Tony glanced at his watch, he was five minutes early.

A strong wind buffered into him from across the Thames. Despite wearing a thick navy-blue goose-down coat, a matching woollen hat, and warm thermal gloves, the cold bit into him hard. He shivered and hunched his shoulders.

Tony looked at his watch again. Just as he thought Stephen wouldn't show up, he heard a voice from behind. 'I'm late. Sorry, mate.'

He turned around. A red-faced Stephen Downer

grinned at him. Like Tony, he was dressed for the cold weather.

'I wanted to say thanks for your help last night. If you hadn't dragged me out of the pub, I'd be in hospital with my dad – or worse.'

Tony shrugged. 'Just trying to do the right thing.'

They walked towards the bridge. Above them, sea gulls swept, making their usual irritating noise. Tony fixed his eyes on the five men approaching from the other side of the river bank, fearing the worst. Stephen might have found out about him standing by while his dad got beaten up, or maybe they were No Mercy. But that made no sense. Why would Stephen work with the people who had put his dad in hospital?

Stephen turned around. 'Don't look so worried, Tony. They're friends.'

They didn't look all that friendly to Tony. 'So, what's all this about?'

'You witnessed my dad getting attacked outside the Libra, didn't you?'

Tony inhaled sharply.

'It wasn't your fault. It would have been stupid to intervene. Most people would have done the same as you.'

He relaxed a little, though his stomach was still churning.

'What I'm about to tell you, you keep to yourself, okay? If you mention it to anyone, you'll be putting other people's lives at risk. So… can I rely on you to keep your mouth shut?'

Tony stepped back, shaking his head 'I don't want any trouble—'

'My dad is on the verge of passing away, and you

were the only witness to the assault. You're involved in this mess whether you like it or not.'

He hadn't mentioned Veronica. He hoped that meant Stephen's source knew nothing about her, and he could keep her from getting dragged into any more of this shit.

'I heard you got a visit from Foster too?'

Tony curled his hands into fists. 'How the fuck could you know about Foster? What's going on here?'

'Don't worry, I'm not going to ask you to inform on Murphy. I want you to join us, help us drive him and the No Mercy firm out of the area for good.'

The five men reached them and clustered around Stephen. They all had stern, soulless faces, which blended in well with the bleak conditions.

'I don't—'

'I wasn't drunk last night. That was an act to draw you in.'

Tony's top lip curled as he resisted the urge to throw a punch at Stephen. 'What the hell is this bollocks? Okay, yes, I saw your dad getting beaten up, but why all this cloak and dagger nonsense? Why me?'

'My dad is on death's door. Which means you and your girlfriend are at risk of having something nasty done to you.'

Tony's breath hitched. That wasn't what he wanted to hear. Bad enough he was involved in this mess, but Veronica didn't deserve any of this. She didn't even live in the area anymore.

'My dad's been receiving information about some of what the No Mercy has been up to. I don't know who informed Murphy.'

Tony scowled, and his impatience grew. 'What information?'

Stephen put his hand in his jacket pocket, as if ready to pull something out. 'Murphy buys drugs in bulk and on the cheap, then he sells it around London and beyond, slapping twenty-five percent on the price he buys it for.'

'What's so shocking about that? That's what criminals do.'

'Yeah, except Murphy's getting his drugs from the Metropolitan Police – at the request of the Home Office.'

'The Home Office?'

'Murphy's got plenty of people on his payroll. It's rumoured he got approached by someone from the Home Office and a senior figure at the Met. They've been selling him the drugs they've seized from police raids while protecting *him* from getting raided. There are warehouses full of government-owned drugs, smuggled into the UK with no customs checks. He's buying all that too.'

'This makes no sense. Why would guardians of law and order want drugs on the street?'

'What do you think'll happen if Britain's streets are full of drugs?'

Tony shrugged, not really sure what Stephen was trying to get him to see.

'It's obvious. They'll put more police on the streets.'

'Maybe.'

'A higher crime rate means more police, which equates to stricter laws. A dictatorship, even.'

'But why create those problems? It will make

everything worse.'

'Because it benefits them to create a lawless Britain with an inept economy. A nation in a state of anarchy requires certain measures to be put in place.'

Tony glanced down at the water and shook his head. 'This is like something out of some conspiracy theory website. I'd go so far as saying this is total bullshit – some sort of wind-up.'

Stephen let off a short, cold laugh. 'I wish it was, but there's a powerful group of people who want Britain to become a totalitarian state, and the No Mercy firm is in the thick of it. Rather than having a multitude of gangs carrying out their dirty work, they have one gang they can keep their eyes on.'

'Okay, so if what you're telling me is true, why do you want me involved? I'm nobody special. This kind of shit is way above me. I work on the railways doing track maintenance. This is fucking bonkers.'

'You think my dad getting bashed to fuck was just used as an opportunity to wind you up? Are you for real? We're talking about my dad. He's in a coma, for fuck's sake!' Stephen's eyes widened, his shoulders hunched upward, and the lines in his forehead deepened. 'We need you for something specific. I can't say what just yet, but we need your help. This is war, Tony. Look at the sacrifice people made during the World Wars. Ordinary people doing extraordinary things.'

Tony leaned against the railings, taking in everything Stephen had said. This was way over his head. He let out a heavy sigh, contemplating his next move. If Stephen was right, things were worse than he thought, but he had Veronica to consider now. He didn't want to drag her into any of this.

Stephen put his arm across Tony's shoulder. 'Let me introduce you to the others. This is Richard Filtness.' He gestured to the man closest to them. 'He's an ex-Royal Marine. Simon Gatting, a freelance journalist. John Bandler, a C.I.D detective; Jim Cranner, a Home Office official; and Bob Davis who's a former member of the SAS.'

Tony nodded at each of the men in turn before facing Stephen. 'How did your dad know all this? I thought he was a painter and decorator.'

Stephen looked ruffled and glanced at his colleagues. Jim, who Tony took to be in his early-forties, smiled. 'That information has to remain a secret, I'm afraid. You'll understand more in due course. You should be grateful Stephen's giving you an insight into the dangers ahead.'

'Yeah,' he said though he felt anything but grateful. Confused, concerned – afraid, even – was more like it.

'I assume after what you've heard you're with us?' Stephen asked.

'I'll think about it.'

Stephen nodded. 'Remember, not a word about this to anyone. If you do, you'll put those people, and yourself, in jeopardy.'

'Yeah.'

The other men turned and walked away. Stephen joined them, leaving Tony alone on the bridge. He wasn't sure he believed them, but they certainly believed it. It was surreal. Stephen was a plumber. How on earth had he got involved with that motley crew? And if what they said *was* true, what could six men possibly do to put things right?

6

Monday morning came around quicker than Tony liked; he liked sitting in a minibus full of track workers even less. Railway track maintenance wasn't the most thought-inspiring work. They were heading to a job in rural Essex, and it already stank of bad breath and stale farts.

Billy Longsmith drove the bus while picking his nose. The radio was tuned into a twenty-four-hour phone-in station about all things football. No one in the minibus looked happy, and enduring football talk was not Tony's idea of fun. 'Do we have to listen to this nonsense, Bill? Any chance of some music?'

Tony doubted Billy had even heard him. He seemed fixated on a discussion about tactics and players not reaching their full potential. Tony thumped the dashboard. 'Oi, turn that nonsense off before we all die of boredom.'

Billy snapped out of his trance. 'What's got into you? You used to love football. You're getting right poncey these days.'

'Yeah, I've noticed that too,' Joe said. 'He thinks he's

above us these days.'

'I just want to listen to some music.'

Despite his protests, the radio remained on the football station. Tony stared out the window. His lips tightened, and he cringed as the radio droned on. He couldn't wait to get his studying up and running so he could leave this job and throw it into the trash can of history. The sooner he got away from these gormless baboons, the better.

Joe had squeezed into the middle seat at the front of the bus. He was like a walking food store. His carrier bag was full of sandwiches, sausage rolls, crisps, and chocolate. He pulled out a sausage roll and munched on it. Even though it was early in the morning, Joe had already raided the carrier bag and was making a right mess of himself. Bits of pastry stuck around his mouth, and he kept farting. With his cropped hair and eighteen stone body, he wasn't a sight to behold.

'Don't you ever stop eating, or farting?' said Tony.

'Shut it, you poncey idiot,' replied Joe, spitting lumps of sausage roll onto Tony's shoulder.

Tony shook his head and stared out of the window again. The emptiness in his stomach grew as he did his best to eradicate the shit floating around his head.

The van pulled up at a set of red traffic lights. Joe slapped Tony's arm and pointed. 'See that building over there?'

Tony glanced over at what looked like a bungalow on the grounds of a hospital. 'What about it?'

'That's the clap clinic. When I was younger, I was over there all the time. I was fucking every woman in sight.' Joe's face screwed up, and bits of sausage roll stuck around his teeth.

'Wow. I take it that makes you the local hero? All those women, eh? Where did it all go wrong, Joe?'

Tony rolled his eyes. In all the time he had known Joe, and despite all the talk about his sexual antics, he had never seen Joe pick up a woman and reasoned that the only woman he could, would be at a brothel.

The lights turned green, and the bus moved off. Tony cringed as football talk turned to stories about how many women his colleagues had had sex with.

Ten minutes later, Billy pulled the bus into the railway car park. 'Here we are, boys and girls. Time to stop scratching your bollocks and get to work on that track,' said Billy.

Moans and yawns echoed around the bus. Each of the men pulled on an orange, high-visibility jacket and a pair of trousers, leaving their white safety helmets until last.

The team entered via the locked metal gate that allowed workers access to the railways and received their assignments for the day. Most of the work was to clear up areas of the track that were untidy and do some shovelling, leaving the main work to be done at night when the tracks shut down for passenger trains.

Tony was lumbered with Joe and Billy, and they set about their tasks, shovelling ballast.

Fifteen minutes passed before Joe stopped shovelling. He took off his white safety helmet and wiped sweat from his brow as he glanced at Billy. 'Blimey, Bill, you look like you're gonna have a heart attack, mate.'

Billy put his shovel down and laughed. 'Heart attack? Are you for real, fat boy? All that crap you shove down

SERFDOM AND DISORDER

your throat and the size of your gut? I don't know how your heart can take another five minutes of this. That's why you've stopped, you lazy git.' He turned to Tony next. 'What happened to Downer on Friday night? It was a good thing you got rid of him. Those No Mercy blokes would have beat him to a bloody pulp.'

'I didn't want to see him get hurt.'

Joe sported a mocking look. 'What are you now, a knight in shining armour? You really aren't yourself anymore. It's that woman you're seeing… what's her name again? Oh, yeah, Veronica.'

Tony tensed. 'Why don't you shut the fuck up?'

'I'll give you a fucking slap, shall I? You don't talk to me like that.'

Tony threw a punch without thinking. Joe staggered backwards, tumbling against a wall. Billy grabbed Tony and held onto him, but Joe was out cold. Tony winced and cradled his right hand as the rest of the work gang dropped their tools and ran towards them.

'You've pushed me too far this time, Joe. I am sick of your constant sniping!' Tony yanked himself free of Billy's grip. 'I'm out of here. Stick this shit job up your arse.'

Tony shoved his way through his colleagues. He marched over ballast and headed towards the exit gate.

Billy ran after him. 'Tony, don't do this. You're upset. You made a mistake. Just stop a minute.'

Tony turned around and shook his head. 'No, that's it for me, Bill. I can't stand this job anymore.'

Joe's eyes fluttered opened; his jaw was already swelling and turning purple. 'You bastard. I'll get you for this,' he slurred.

Tony glared at him. 'Fuck off.'

He stormed towards the exit gate, still holding his throbbing hand. A weird sensation with colours swirling all around overtook him. When he blinked, he found himself outside a hospital, in the Accident and Emergency car park. His left hand was bandaged, but he had no recollection of getting there or receiving treatment. He glanced at his watch – nine hours had come and gone.

A car horn sounded, startling him. He turned around and there, in her Audi TT Coupe, was Veronica. She lowered the passenger window. 'Are you getting in? You looked as if you were somewhere else.'

'Have you been waiting long?'

'About five minutes.'

Tony eased into the passenger seat, and she drove off with a slight screeching sound from the back tyres. He stared out the window, trying to figure out what the hell was going on. The missing time was freaking him out, and he couldn't tell Veronica because she'd think he was crazy.

'So, I take it you'll be off sick for a few weeks. Perhaps the rest will do you good?'

Tony forced a smile. There was no way he could tell her about the fight, or that he'd walked out of his job and had no idea what he would do next. He had worked in railway track maintenance since leaving school at sixteen and had no experience in anything else. Sure, he was about to start college in a couple of weeks, but that was part-time. It would be a long, hard road before he graduated with a degree, and now he'd made himself unemployed. The prospect of not getting any unemployment benefit, sent a shiver down his spine. He was in deep crap.

'You're in your somewhere-else-mode again, Tony. What's wrong?'

'Just tired. It's been a nightmare of a day. One I'd rather forget.' No sooner had he spoken, his phone rang. 'Stephen?' he said, answering the call.

'Can you meet me in an hour, at my place?'

Tony cringed. He hadn't expected to hear from him so soon and had planned to spend the evening with Veronica curled up on the sofa, watching TV.

'Er, er, yeah, okay, I can do that.'

'Dirleton Road. Number fifty-three.'

'No problem, Stephen. I'll see you there.'

Veronica stopped at traffic lights and glanced at Tony. 'What is it now?'

'Stephen Downer wants to see me about something.'

She produced what looked like a strained smile. 'I assume you'll be seeing *him* tonight then?'

'Yeah, I'm sorry. He's going through hell at the minute, what with his dad – well, you know.' It was the best Tony could come up, and it wasn't far from the truth.

Veronica didn't answer. She pressed her foot on the accelerator as the traffic lights turned green, then slammed her breaks on as another car drove across her from the other direction. Tony grimaced and stroked her arm. She hasn't mentioned anything more about that night at the pub, and he hadn't wanted to bring it up either. As far as she was aware, the unpleasantness was over, with the exception of him continuing to 'support' Stephen Downer.

'Do you want a lift?' she said in a stiff tone.

'I'm really sorry, love. I couldn't tell him to piss off, could I?'

Again, Veronica didn't answer. There was an icy silence between them. Business with Stephen Downer was starting to mess up his life.

'Veronica, I want to be with you tonight more than anything. I'm not pleased about what's happening, but what can I do?'

A smile broke out on Veronica's face. 'Depends on how you intend to make it up.'

Tony grinned. 'Fish and chips?'

'It had better not be! I've driven all this way to pick you up. You're not treating me like a fool. If that's the best you can do, I'll stop this car right now and you can get out and walk!'

Tony's eyebrows raised. He'd never seen Veronica so angry. He caressed her arm again. 'Eh, steady on, I was only having a joke. Of course I don't mean it.'

'I'm not in the mood for games. I've been good to you, Tony. The least you can do is show me some respect.'

7

Tony wanted answers, like how Stephen's dad had received information about Murphy and how Stephen was connected to the team of people he'd introduced him to. The people on the bridge didn't seem the type to mix with a plumber.

He sat in a comfy seat in Stephen Downer's brightly lit but plain-styled living room. A photo of Stephen and his dad holding a huge fish with the sea as a backdrop adorned the sideboard, capturing that perfect father-son moment. Tony's lips tightened as flashes of Stephen's dad being attacked came back to him. He clasped his hands together.

Stephen entered the living room with a cup of tea. He smiled at Tony as he handed it to him. 'We'll be heading into Holborn soon. A friend of ours lets us use an office there. Are you okay with that?'

'Er, yeah.'

The secrecy was making him uncomfortable. He still didn't know what he was getting involved in – or if he should. He needed some answers before he made a decision.

Stephen's mobile rang. Tony's jaw tightened as he looked at him. Stephen answered the call and then gestured for Tony to follow him. 'The car's outside.'

Tony gulped down his tea and stood to leave, a little annoyed at himself for not asking any questions yet. He followed Stephen out to a blue Mercedes C-Class saloon with darkened windows.

Stephen opened the car door and gestured for Tony to get in. Tony looked for some reassurance from him, but what he got was a stone-cold stare. He stepped forward, treading on a half empty can of beer. The contents leaked over his shoe and the bottom of his jeans.

'Shit! Can you ask the driver if he's got anything to wipe this with?'

Stephen pulled a face. The driver tossed a dirty rag towards Tony, who grabbed it and rubbed his shoe. When he finished, he threw it back at the driver in the same stroppy manner and then sunk into the smooth leather seats in the back of the car. There was a car showroom smell about it. Butterflies fluttered in his stomach as his breathing quickened.

The car pulled away from the kerb with the same sensation as a boat on a calm sea. Tony pondered about what he had let himself in for. He wasn't in the mood to talk, so he stared out of the window instead. The smell of beer reeked from his shoe, mingling with the scent of fresh leather in the car.

Stephen scratched the stubble on his chin. 'You've gone quiet, Tony. There's nothing to worry about. When we arrive at Holborn, you can ask whatever you want, but until then' – he reached into a concealed compartment – 'have a shot of this. It'll sort you out.'

He produced a silver flask as new looking as the leather seats. Tony snatched it out of Stephen's hand and took a swig. His eyes lit up, and he coughed as the strong, burning taste of molasses and vanilla flowed down his throat.

'What the hell is that stuff?'

Stephen grinned. 'Eighty percent proof Jamaican rum. I bet that's cleared your head.'

Tony poured another shot down his throat; the fire from it burned through his body.

Stephen took the flask out of Tony's hand. 'Calm it down. We don't want you drunk before the meeting, do we?'

The rum warmed Tony's body and mind, and he felt a lot more confident about the challenges coming his way. The uncertainty had gone, as well as the other issues that had been bothering him too. 'When the meeting's over, perhaps you can get me a bottle of that? It hits the mark.'

'Let's get the meeting over with first, shall we? Though I suppose you'll want to drown your sorrows after the day you've had. Damage your hand, lose your job, and then you end up lumbered with me instead of a night in with Veronica. Am I right?'

'How the hell do you know—'

Stephen put his index finger to his lips. 'Everything will become clearer at the meeting. Enjoy the ride. Relax. Go to sleep, if you want, but no more questions.'

Tony's uneasiness returned as the buzz of alcohol faded. Stephen came across as warm and welcoming, but everything about this was vague. Tony kept fidgeting – first with his feet, then with his thumbs, conscious of Stephen watching him.

The Mercedes eventually reached its destination. Tony got out of the car and looked up at the tall, grand stone building before them. A sense of foreboding washed over him, but it was too late to pull out now.

They took the lift to the seventh floor, and Stephen led the way through a brightly lit corridor of wooden and glass doors. They arrived at an empty reception area, and Tony settled into one of the black leather seats and glanced around. Modern art pictures were scattered around, as well as tropical plants in huge vases.

'I'm bursting for a piss. I'll be back in a minute,' said Stephen as he walked out of the reception area through another set of doors.

A nerve twitched in the corner of Tony's mouth. Stephen had said there would be other people at the meeting, but there was nobody else here. He imagined Murphy's heavies bursting through the door to drag him away. When the door swung open, he jumped halfway out his skin but relaxed when he recognised the man as Richard Filtness, the ex-Royal Marine. He looked like a city stockbroker in his office attire: a white shirt, blue silk tie, dark grey trousers, and shiny black slip-on shoes. Tony reckoned him to be in his late forties with his trendy, short-cropped grey hair.

Richard shook Tony's hand with a firm grip, coming across as cold and serious, reinforced by his round, steel rimmed spectacles. His face gave nothing away. 'Would you like to follow me, Tony?'

'What about Stephen? Shouldn't we wait for him?'

'It's okay. He knows what room we're in.'

SERFDOM AND DISORDER

Tony followed Richard through the door. The staff who usually occupied the open-plan office had long-since gone home. Richard led him towards a partitioned room on the opposite side. The Venetian blinds were shut closed over the clear glass windows, but Tony could just make out the light from inside.

Richard opened the door, stood aside, and gestured for Tony to enter. The other men who Tony had met on the Connaught Bridge, were sitting along a vertical table littered with paperwork and vending machine cups. Each one of them was dressed in a shirt and tie. No pleasantries were exchanged, just nods of acknowledgement.

'Would you like a cup of tea or coffee from our wonderful vending machine?' asked Simon Gatting, the journalist, if Tony recalled rightly.

'Yeah, cheers.'

Tony slipped into a seat, ignoring the paperwork in front of him for the moment.

Stephen entered the room and apologised for being late. He appeared embarrassed, judging from the red glow on his face, and slipped into a seat beside Richard.

Richard fixed his gaze on Tony. 'I'll bet you're bemused about all this? Let's hope this meeting will give you an insight into what we're planning.'

'Let's hope so,' Tony said. 'No pussy-footing around. Give it to me straight.'

Richard nodded. 'The No Mercy firm, as they like to call themselves, operate out of Canning Town. They control most of East London now. No one stands against them. But Murphy's ready to spread his tentacles further afield, and now he's got the backing of the

Home Office and the Met, there'll be no stopping him.'

Tony shuffled in his seat. 'You said that already, but unless I see some pictures or documents, or whatever it is you've got to prove all this, I'm off. I'm not going to be taken for a fool.'

John Bandler rose from his seat and tossed a brown paper file towards Tony. The CID man cracked his knuckles. 'Well, go on then, have a look. That should stop your paranoia.'

Tony sat upright and stared into John's eyes. 'Paranoia? You've asked me to join you. I've got every right to question what's being said.'

'So I suppose you'll be thinking that file is fake – compiled to manipulate you?'

Tony stood up, pointing his finger at John. 'Who do you think you are to speak to me like this? I'm here because you want me for whatever it is you want me for. What you've told me so far has piqued my curiosity, but I don't need any pressure from you, John. It's out of order.'

Other members from the group rose from their seats. One of the men spoke to John, while Jim Cranner, the Home Office official, sat Tony back down. 'Just look at the file, Tony. See what you think.'

Tony opened the folder and looked through the photos. One of them showed Shaun Murphy sitting next to two men dressed in senior police uniforms. There was some paperwork – copies of emails – outlining meetings between Murphy and shadowy members of the Home Office. The details of their plan to bring anarchy to London and the Home Counties, and then the entire country, weren't entirely apparent.

SERFDOM AND DISORDER

Tony looked up, scratched his head, and sighed. 'To be honest, the text messages and the emails can be faked. The photos, too.'

John shook his head. 'Ask yourself why a common criminal is sitting laughing and speaking with senior members of the police force.' He leaned across the table and slid one of the photos out of the pile. 'That's the Chief Constable for crissake, and this one,' he said, dragging another photo free, 'he's in charge of Scotland Yard.'

'The thinkers behind the Home Office and the Met are helping Murphy further his aims,' Richard said. 'He's been receiving everything he needs to make his ambition a reality – drugs, guns, and opportunities for a multitude of rackets.'

Tony rubbed his hands together, staring intently at Richard.

'They want anarchy, Tony. Once Murphy's wiped out the rival gangs and got the monopoly – and those drugs hit the streets – and the public cry out for tougher police measures, they'll make their move. This goes all the way to the top. Britain is going to plunge into chaos. Unless *we* do something about it.'

A phone rang, and Richard rolled his eyes. Bob dug his hand into his pocket with a sheepish grin. 'Sorry, Rich, I'll turn it off.'

Richard waited for him to do that and then continued. 'We heard about the plan from a reliable source. They intend to introduce martial law eventually, and once that's in place, the more draconian measures will go ahead. There's even talk of labour camps because by then, there'll be a lack of jobs. Food rationing has been discussed, too. In effect, Britain will not only be a police state; it'll become a nation of serfs.'

Tony rolled his eyes. 'No one is going to issue instructions for anyone to live in a system like that.'

'You'd think so, wouldn't you? But there's an organisation behind all this. It's not just the Home Office and the Met involved. There's a group of freemasons running this. They call themselves the 1066 group, so-called for the date when the Normans first invaded these shores. They're direct descendants of Norman lords, as far as we can tell. Most of their members are ultra-rich, very powerful, and they want a Norman feudal system in place.'

'That's ridiculous. They—'

'Murphy's already begun his reign of terror. You won't have seen anything about that in the media because they control that too, but murders amongst the criminal faction are up three-fold.'

Stephen stood up. 'Truth is, Tony, my dad was an undercover journalist. He presented himself to the local community as a painter and decorator to check out Shaun Murphy. He kept hearing rumours about him. Unfortunately for my dad, he unravelled a web that put him in hospital. I'm a freelance journalist too. My being a plumber is a perfect cover. I never worked with my dad. I run an online blog. I've got my own contacts and leads for stories.'

Tony took a gulp of coffee from his plastic cup. 'How did you know about the shit between me and Joe?'

'Er, well, to be honest, Joe's on our payroll for different matters. He's clueless about our activities. We told Joe to wind you up so you'd hit him.'

'So I'm out of a fucking job because of you? This is my life we're talking about.'

'Yeah, we're sorry about that, but there was a reason for it.'

'What's that then? Got a top job lined up for me somewhere? I've got rent to pay, you know. Bills and shit.'

Stephen grinned. 'Actually we have – a job that is. The 1066 group have a gentleman's club in the city of London. There's a vacancy at the club. As a waiter."

'You're having a fucking laugh, aren't you? A waiter!'

'Don't worry, the pay's good in these clubs.'

'Except I've got no experience in that line of work.'

'Yeah, which is why we arranged a crash course for you in a restaurant in Plaistow during the weekend. After that, you'll be a first-class waiter, butler, and valet, all rolled into one.'

Tony shook his head. 'You set me up and then expect me to become a fucking butler at a dodgy Freemason's club? And besides,' he said, raising his arm, 'I can't arrive for work with my hand bandaged up, can I?'

'No, you can't. The dressing will have to come off before you go to work.'

'Not giving it much of a chance to heal then, am I?'

'The alternative is that, you, Veronica, and everyone else you love, could end up in a work camp. Is that what you want, Tony'

'Of course not.' He stared at the blinds. Everything was happening too fast. He wasn't cut out to be a hero in the pages of a history book, but he couldn't bear the thought of being stuck in a work camp either.

'Are you okay, Tony? I know it's a lot to take in, but you're a part of this organisation now, and we've all got a part to play. This isn't easy for any of us.'

'Hang on a second. I haven't agreed to this yet.'

He glanced around at each of the men. They seemed genuine enough, and he couldn't see them going to the trouble of faking the contents in the file for his sake. He was no one special. There was nothing he had that they could want. Plus, he needed to keep himself and Veronica safe, *and* he needed a job, as shitty as working as a waiter sounded.

'Count me in,' he said finally. 'But you better be right about the pay at that club. You owe me.'

The men offered outstretched hands and patted him on the back.

'You won't regret this,' Stephen said.

'I hope not, but what about the rest of you? What are *your* motives for getting involved in all this?'

Richard twiddled with his ear before sitting upright. 'I fought in Afghanistan and Iraq, amongst other places, and I'm fucked if I'm going to let the 1066 group turn Britain into a state of servitude. I helped Charles – Stephen's dad – with an undercover story in the past, and we kept in contact. When Stephen told me what had happened and what else was going on, I had to get involved.'

'Me and Charles go way back. We've been working on this story together for some time now,' Simon said.

Jim lifted his head from the paperwork on the desk. 'I work with the Home Office, or rather, I did. I blew the lid off what was going on. I stumbled across some of their files and once I realised what was happening, I approached Stephen's dad. I've fed him other stories over the years too.'

John stood up next, pulling on his coat. 'I'm CID. I've been investigating Murphy for several years. One of my informants introduced me to Stephen, and matters evolved from there. It sickens me that the Force is involved in this.'

Bob Davis was the last to speak. He leaned across the table and stared at Tony. 'I met Simon while on duty on a mission in Africa. He was there with a load of other journos. We kept in touch, meeting up for a beer or two. When he informed me about Murphy and these other forces, I was shocked. I want to get back at these people who want to destroy my country.'

Tony gave a curt nod to everyone, and then they went their separate ways. Tony caught the tube back to Plaistow with Stephen. He felt a little happier now he understood the situation and why each member had got involved, though he was a little unsure of what he could contribute to the team.

He glanced around the carriage. The few people on it looked bored. Tony glanced at Stephen. 'I thought you were trying to set me up, punishing me for what happened to your dad, what with me not helping him out.'

'Murphy's a heavy-duty gangster. If you had helped, you wouldn't be sitting here now.'

8

The weekend drifted to a close. Tony had finished his short training course in serving and now sat in a plush Italian restaurant with Veronica. The atmosphere was relaxing, full of couples and larger groups talking quietly amongst themselves. The lighting was dim and a soft, and a mellow jazz-funk soundtrack played in the background.

Tony knocked back his glass of Jack Daniels. He was dreading starting the job at the 1066 club. The clientele who attended that sort of place weren't his favourite kind of human beings. He despised the arrogance that came from people born into wealth. He also felt the need to get just a little bit drunk. It burned his throat and went straight to his brain. Food stuck to his chin as he ate, and he couldn't stop his childish giggling.

Veronica gave Tony a cool, hard stare. 'Don't you think you've had enough to drink? You're fast becoming like all those other idiots you associate with.'

Her scathing words were enough to snap him out of his stupidity. He took a drink of water, eager to sober up – and fast.

'I'm sorry,' Tony slurred. 'I've been an idiot. I just fancied getting a little tipsy is all'

'Whatever's bothering you… I can help, if you'd talk to me.'

Tony stared at her. 'I didn't want to tell you, but I'm starting a new job tomorrow evening at a gentlemen's club in the City.'

'What was so hard about telling me that?' She smiled. 'That's a big change from working on the railways. What's brought that about?'

'I bumped into someone from my school days. We got chatting about different things. I told him how much I hated my job, and he gave me a number to call. The rest is history.'

'Yes, but why that? Your views about the City and its financial institutions are… a bit extreme. It's an odd career change.'

Veronica was sharp. He poured another glass of water from the jug to give himself time to think and gulped it.

'He, er, he said working there would increase my chances of getting a better job. Said I could make contacts. I couldn't turn that down, could I?'

Veronica smiled. She appeared to approve and took his hand in hers. 'I'm pleased for you. It sounds like a good move. In fact, Tony Harrison, I'm very proud of you. Now I can understand why you're drinking so much. You're apprehensive, aren't you?'

Tony smiled. He was so grateful to be with this lovely woman, and he hated the lies he kept churning out. If she found out the truth, it would kill their relationship.

J.P. GADSTON

He glanced around the restaurant and caught sight of a face he recognized from the local paper, a rival of the No Mercy firm if he wasn't mistaken. Tony's stomach tightened as he watched him eat.

Veronica's mouth sagged. 'Do you know him?'

Tony put a finger to his lips. 'Shhh.'

He scanned the restaurant to see if there were any other gangster types around. When a waiter walked through the kitchen door, Tony sat up straight. He wasn't a waiter Tony had seen so far, and he couldn't shake off the feeling that something wasn't right.

'I think we should go,' Tony said.

'What do you mean?'

'Something bad is going down. I want us out of here.'

'That drink's done something to your brain.'

Tony stood up. 'We need to go – now.'

'I can't believe I'm hearing this. I was looking forward to dessert. Where's all this paranoia coming from?'

'Veronica, please. Not now.'

She stood up abruptly and threw her napkin on her plate. 'I'll fetch the coats then, shall I?'

Veronica stormed off to the cloak room as Tony settled the bill at the payment desk. A movement caught the corner of Tony's eye, and he turned to see the waiter pulling out a pistol and firing at the No Mercy rival. The man slumped face-first into his dinner plate.

Screams filled the restaurant as panic descended. People jumped from their chairs and ran for the exit. Veronica was just leaving the cloak room. She wore hers and carried Tony's over her arm. Tony grabbed her and hurried her outside.

'What's happening?' Veronica asked as he hurried

her along. 'First that man gets beaten close to death and now this.'

Tony's insides tightened. 'Come on. Let's get out of here before the police arrive. There's no way I want to answer questions about this.'

Veronica tugged against Tony's hand. 'You knew this would happen, didn't you?'

'We can talk about it when we get back to my place.'

They flagged a passing black taxi and jumped in the back. Veronica was trembling, and Tony put an arm around her, cuddling up close and did his best to keep her calm on the short journey home.

When the taxi pulled into the Rawstone Walk car park, they got out and headed towards the stairwell.

'Well, that's one good thing,' Veronica said.

'One good thing, what?'

'The stairwell's empty.'

Tony smiled. He didn't explain why it was empty or his role in it.

Once they were back in his flat, Tony got their drinks out of the refrigerator. Veronica smiled a bitter smile.

Her eyes fixed on his. 'Tony, what happened tonight? How did you guess what would happen?'

'It was a hunch.'

'What do you mean?'

'I recognised the man who got shot. He's an enemy of the No Mercy firm. When the waiter came out of the kitchen, my gut told me something wasn't right. I'm glad we left when we did. I didn't fancy getting caught up in that.'

'Why does this keep happening to us?'

Tony shook his head. 'I don't know, but we're safe now.'

9

Veronica went home in the early hours of Monday morning, leaving Tony to sit in the kitchen, yawning and daydreaming while the radio played in the background. He caressed his unshaven face, trying to find the motivation to get ready for his first shift at the 1066 club.

His mobile phone rang and he glanced at the screen before answering. 'Hello, Stephen, what's up?'

'You out of bed?'

'Yeah.'

'Good, because I'm just walking up your stairwell. Get the kettle on; I'm gasping for a cup of tea.'

Moments later, the doorbell rang. Stephen grinned and stepped inside. 'All set for your new job?'

'I'm not thrilled about it, but yeah, I'm ready.'

Tony led Stephen into the kitchen, filled the kettle with water, and flicked the switch.

'The service in this place isn't much cop,' said Stephen. 'You'll be losing a star over this.'

'Is this the fucking Michelin Guide or something?'

SERFDOM AND DISORDER

Stephen laughed. 'Did you hear about that gangster getting shot up last night?'

'I was there.'

'What?'

'I was having a meal with Veronica, but we didn't hang around.'

'I heard it was a No Mercy hit.'

Tony placed a cup of tea in front of him. 'Maybe.'

'What we've been telling you is coming to fruition. We expect lots of gangsters to get executed in the coming weeks.'

'It's odd though, isn't it? He was on enemy territory. You would have thought he'd know better.'

Stephen shrugged. 'Must have got lured there. Perhaps by someone from higher up.'

'It spoiled my night with Veronica.'

Stephen stood up and unzipped his goose-down coat. He put his hand inside his jacket pocket and pulled out a metallic device with a wire attached to it. 'You'll be wearing one of these at the club. It'll pick up anything they're saying, so long as you get close enough to the right people. A lot of what they say is in code. It's a Freemason's club; what else do you expect? They have their own language, though fortunately for us, we've cracked it.'

He slid the device across the table. 'When you start your shift, you'll get shown to the changing room. Your uniform will be in your locker, along with a device just like this, but don't put it on in there. There's CCTV. You're better off going into the toilets to do that.'

He gave Tony a quick demonstration of how to position the device inside his coat.

'Once you've finished your shift, leave the device in your locker.'

Tony took a sip of tea. 'I'm sure I'll be fine. I've got the first day jitters, but doesn't everyone?' he said, sounding a lot more confident than he felt.

Before all the business with Murphy and the 1066 group started, he knew Stephen well enough to share a nod of acknowledgement, but that was about it. Over the last couple of days, he had got to know him a little better. He admired the way he was holding up with his dad in such a critical condition and his drive to bring about the downfall of the 1066 group. Tony had mixed emotions about his involvement. One side of him viewed it as his moral duty to protect Veronica and everyone else he cared for from the threat posed by the 1066 group. The other side – his anxious side – screamed at him not to get involved, to let it be someone else's problem.

Tony stared at Stephen. 'Wouldn't it be better to go public about this? If they had even the slightest awareness of what was going on—'

Stephen shook his head. 'It would sound too much like a conspiracy theory. They'd never believe us, assuming we could get the story out in the first place.'

Tony sighed. 'If we fail, the consequences don't bear thinking about.'

'Your role at the club is vital. We need as much intel as we can get. If the club starts dragging your spirits down, just remind yourself why you're there.' He gulped the last of his tea down and stood up. 'Thanks for the tea. I'll catch up with you later, yeah?'

Stephen shook hands with Tony and let himself out

as Tony flicked the kettle back on and made himself another cup of tea. He assumed they had someone else in the club and kicked himself for not asking more questions. He glanced at his mobile but dismissed the idea of ringing Stephen to ask. Whoever it was would be as much a part of the team as he was, though it begged the question of why they couldn't use them to do the spy work.

He stared at the washing machine and yawned. There wasn't much else to do, so he headed back to bed. He needed sleep.

He woke not long after four o'clock. By five, he was sitting on a District Line train, heading to Mile End station. He stared out at the familiar landscape as it passed, most of which was overground. His phone rang, and he fumbled to answer it under the scrutiny of the other passengers. It was Veronica calling to wish him luck.

'I'm fine,' he assured her.

'Oh, I am pleased. After the way you were drinking last night, I thought you would be too hungover today. I can hear train noise. Are you at the station?'

'I'm on the District Line train. Not far to go now. A quick change at Mile End to the Central Line and then onto Bank. The club's just around the corner.'

'Okay, my sweet, I'll see you during the week, if I can? Love you.'

'I love you too, sweetheart. Bye.'

He glanced around the train, but nobody looked his way. Their lifeless grey faces seemed to be elsewhere.'

At Mile End station, the Central Line train arrived with a loud clatter. As Tony was about to board, he noticed a pale-looking man with combed forward, light blond hair. He wore a tight black jumpsuit and was acting a little strange. He looked like he was having a conversation with the back of the person in front of him. What was stranger still was that no one was paying him any attention.

The carriage doors closed, and the train set off again. Colours flashed before Tony's eyes. He closed them for a moment, and when he opened them again, the strange-looking man was right beside him. 'What the hell?'

The passengers closest to him turned and stared. A mad screaming roared inside his head, and he gripped the handhold above his head until his knuckles turned white. The strange-looking man leaned forward. 'Have you noticed that you haven't had any unusual experiences of late?'

Tony's jaw dropped open. Who the hell was that, and how did he know about the weird experiences? 'I—'

'No! Don't speak aloud. This lot will think you're crazy.' He gestured to the surrounding passengers. 'Speak through your mind. I'll be able to hear you.'

Tony squeezed his eyes shut and shook his head, but the man was still there when he opened them again.

'There's nothing to worry about, Tony. Communication broke down between us. Bit of a glitch at our end, but I think we've sorted it out now. You might have experienced some distortions too, time jumps and whatnot. Anyway, I just wanted to make sure you're okay. We don't have long. It's still a bit temperamental. So, are you o—'

The man disappeared before he could finish his

sentence. Tony glanced at the other passengers, wondering if they had seen any of that, but no one glanced in his direction. They were either staring at their reflection in the train windows or engrossed in their mobile phones, books, or newspapers.

Just as Tony got his head together, the train pulled into Bank Station. It was as if he had only been on the train for a few minutes, but the normal journey from Mile End was about fifteen minutes. Sweat trickled down his brow. He leaned against the train doors as his heart pounded. He couldn't blame this experience on skunk weed smoke. Maybe it was his anxiety, but he couldn't recall hallucinating because of it before.

Tony emerged from the station at street level and followed the GPS on his phone to Cornhill. The closer he got to the club, the more the trepidation set in.

The 1066 club was located in a street of Victorian stone buildings against a backdrop of glass-and-steel office blocks. A real combination of the old and the new.

Butterflies formed in Tony's stomach as he approached the main entrance. The building stood out amongst all the other dire, soulless, architectural drivel. Its decadence was homage to the Victorian era's architecture, with influences from the Roman Empire thrown in too. Stone pillars on either side of the black marble stairway lead up to the main entrance and an oversized door.

Tony felt a presence behind him and turned around. There, across the road, stood the man in the black jumpsuit. He blinked, and the man was suddenly beside him. Tony stumbled backwards, hitting his head on one of the stone pillars. 'What the fuck!' *Who is this bloke?*

The strange man smiled. 'Just hold it together, and remember to—'

The man disappeared again. Tony shook his head and turned to the shiny black doors of the club. He took a deep breath, putting the weird experience behind him, and depressed the gold-coloured metal doorbell with a trembling hand.

A man who looked in his early sixties opened the door. He wore the staff club uniform: white shirt; black tie; red waistcoat with silver buttons; a long, dark green coat; black trousers; and black shoes. It was as if he'd come from another century. The shine from the man's bald head glowed beneath the lighting. Tony frowned. He could just imagine Veronica falling on the floor with laughter if she ever saw *him* dressed like that.

'Can I help you?' the man asked, sounding like a butler from a period drama.

'Er, yeah. My name's Tony Harrison. I'm starting here today as a waiter.'

'Oh, yes, the new boy. Come in.'

Tony entered the lobby, and the man shut the door behind him. A short distance ahead was another set of large black doors and two stairwells, one leading to the left and the other to the right. There was also what looked like an X-ray machine. It had two panels on both sides and a path that ran in-between. Tony walked through the centre while the bald-headed man stood on the other side of the panel.

'You can go through now.'

Tony glanced at the interior. A beautiful mural of a rural scene adorned the high ceiling. It looked like a

SERFDOM AND DISORDER

scene from Norman England. Similar scenes from Old England, with writing in Latin, impressed on his vision. He reflected on how out of place he was in such an establishment.

Glass chandeliers hung from other parts of the ceiling, reflecting off the white marble flooring. Everywhere he looked had a sense of pomp and grandiosity.

At ground level stood smaller doors on either side, also painted black. It was exactly how he imagined a freemason's club in the City of London to look. There was also the subtle scent of rose that added to the atmospherics.

'This way, please, Mr Harrison.' The man led the way and Tony followed. His guts churned as his nerves increased his adrenaline levels.

The man led him through a green baize side door on the right and along a corridor of plain-looking and uninviting dark walls. There were no pictures here, and it had an old, worn black carpet.

'I take it this is the area reserved for the staff?' said Tony. The man stared at him without a hint of emotion, clearly devoid of a sense of humour.

The aroma of delicious food wafted out of the kitchen as they passed. His mouth watered, though he doubted the staff would get any of the food. He would probably have to bring in his own sandwiches.

They stopped outside another green door. 'This is the changing room, Mr Harrison. Locker number seventeen is yours. Here's the key. You will find your uniform inside. Once you are dressed, report to the office three doors along. Oh, and I am the staff manager. My name is Mr Hayes.'

J.P. GADSTON

'How did you know my size... for my uniform?'

'We have our way of doing things here, Mr Harrison. You don't have to worry about the how of it all.'

Mr Hayes turned and walked away. Tony entered the changing room, mimicking Hayes's response under his breath. *Snobby git.*

Tony located his locker and unlocked the padlock. The door swung open, and he stared at the uniform hanging inside. It was identical to Mr Hayes's. If the people he'd worked with on the railways saw him in it, he'd never live it down. Fortunately, there was no chance of *that* ever happening.

He changed with his back to the CCTV camera, studying his reflection in the wall mirror when he was finished. He giggled. He resembled one of Santa's helpers, minus the pointed hat and elf ears. His sombre mood returned when he slipped his hand inside the pocket of the long green coat and touched what he assumed was the bugging device.

Tony put the padlock back on his locker and set off to find the toilets so he could put on the bugging device. As he stepped into the corridor, he saw a member of staff dressed in the same uniform approaching. When he reached Tony, he shook his hand. 'David Ryder,' he said, introducing himself.

'Tony Harrison. Don't suppose you can point me in the direction of the loo? I'm bursting.'

'Sure, but don't take too long. Mr Hayes doesn't like staff loitering in there for any length of time.'

Tony scowled as he followed David's directions to the toilets. He didn't like the vibes in the club. David made it sound as if he'd have to ask permission every time he wanted to take a piss.

He stepped inside one of the cubicles and hung up his coat on the hook inside the toilet door before he pulled out the bugging device. His hands shook as he fumbled to switch it on, and he had to stop to take a breath to calm himself. He listened to make sure no one had entered the toilet area and then uttered a few soft words into the device. 'You bastards better be listening. I don't want to go through this crap for nothing.'

Once the device was secure, he headed to Mr Hayes's office. Tony straightened his uniform and knocked on the door. When Mr Hayes answered, Tony stepped inside.

Mr Hayes looked up at him. 'Take a seat please, Mr Harrison. I want to give you a few rules and regulations that this club expects from its staff.'

Tony sat awkwardly. It brought back memories of being summoned to the headmaster's office for misbehavior in class.

Mr Hayes informed him of the standards he expected his staff to adhere to. His tone was dull and monotonous. Fine in small doses, but that was about it. His face was stern, too, and he had a sickly, pale look about him. He appeared to get off on preaching the rules, which only added to Mr Hayes's lack of charm. The more he droned on, the more Tony's resentment built. The bloke was an eccentric – more than a bit nutty. Every employee understood they shouldn't arrive late for work and how to behave *in* work. It seemed to Tony that the man was on a power trip, and he was a fucking moron at that.

'Okay, Mr Harrison.' He rose from his chair. 'Come

with me, and I shall show you where our members congregate. At the moment, only staff will be there. Members arrive from six o'clock onwards.'

He led Tony to one of the rooms down the stairs. Tony entered with no idea of what to expect. The first thing that greeted him was the smell. It had a distinct aroma of peaches, and it gave the room a different characteristic to the rose scent from the reception area. The thick, dark green carpet blended with the brown leather Chesterfield sofas and chairs.

As in the foyer, pictures of rural scenes from the Norman period hung on oak-panelled walls. The room oozed with comfort, a place where members of the gentlemen's club could unwind after a day of work in the City.

Mr Hayes fixed Tony with a glare. 'You won't be working upstairs just yet. You will familiarise yourself with the workings of this room first. In time, you might receive clearance, but at the moment, upstairs is off limits to you.'

'Why do I have to have clearance for that, then?'

Mr Hayes didn't answer. Curiosity piqued Tony's interest. He wondered how long he would have to work here before being allowed upstairs, assuming he could stand being here for any length of time. He'd had more than enough of the place already.

Tony smiled weakly, acknowledging Mr Hayes's instructions with a nod.

For his first role, he was to serve the gentlemen drinks and whatever food they had ordered. He stood rigid against the oak-panelled wall. The palm of his better hand held out a silver tray. He felt completely humiliated.

Club members trickled in, dressed formally in shirts, ties, and suits. Some club members either smirked or sneered, others had direct probing eye contact. A lot of the members appeared drunk upon arrival; their faces bright red, and there was a distinct smell of booze surrounding them. They stumbled as they attempted to walk around the member's area.

No doubt these idiots had been boozing since finishing their "hard shift" at the Stock Exchange, or wherever they worked, while Tony stood at the side like a boy from a Victorian workhouse.

A red-faced member in a green tweed jacket, light blue shirt, and yellow silk tie focused on Tony. He clicked his fingers. 'Come here, boy.'

Tony approached him, appearing calm on the outside but burning with anger within.

'Get me a gin and tonic, and make it quick. I'm thirsty.'

'Yes, sir.'

He gritted his teeth and walked to the dark oak wooden paneled bar. He felt ready to explode and would think nothing at smashing the silver platter over the man's head. Who did these people think they were?

Tony served the member his gin and tonic. The man snatched it and dismissed him with a wave of his hand. Tony returned to the wall, waiting for his next order. He avoided looking at the members directly. They infuriated him. He just hoped the bugging device was picking up the conversation, that something of use could be taken from it, and that this would be the one and only time he'd be expected to work here.

J.P. GADSTON

'I hear that a lot of workers are demanding pay rises. I thought we put a stop to that. What is the point of legislation if it works against us? We should freeze our donations to the government for a time. That will let them know we are serious.'

'The correct thing to do is to get our lobbying representatives together and approach the Prime Minister.'

Drunken laughter roared across the tables as the night dragged on. The noise level increased with every round of drinks. Laughter and shouting was dressed up in arrogant tones as the members waved their arms about in heated debates. One of Tony's colleagues got called over to serve a member. A man in his forties with dark, thick, side-parted hair, snapped his fingers continuously. 'Come here, you fucking imbecile. I want a drink – now!' He slammed the palm of his hand on the adjoining small table with force. 'Come on, you fucking goon, get me my drink!'

Tony's brow deepened as another member clicked his fingers in Tony's direction – the man he had first served. 'Get me a drink. The same as before.'

Tony took deep breaths as he approached the bar, somehow calming himself down. He served the man his drink and retreated to the wall. It didn't sound as if there was much coded talk going on, and there was absolutely no mention of Murphy or their plan. The real Freemason stuff probably went on upstairs, which raised the question of why he was even here.

When the shift finally ended, Tony stepped out into the empty, freezing streets, grateful to have made it through the shift without punching anyone. A black cat hissed, its fangs on display. Tony jolted and walked around it. It was three in the morning. There were no tube trains, which meant he'd have to rough it on the night bus.

He yearned to get home and return to some normality. He longed for the comfort of his flat, relaxing in front of the TV.

'You want a lift home, Tony?'

It was David Ryder, the staff member he had met briefly. Tony had been so engrossed in his thoughts he hadn't noticed the silver Peugeot pulling up alongside him.

'Come on, get in. Don't stand out in the freezing cold for too long.'

Tony smiled, relieved he didn't need to catch the night bus. He opened the passenger door and got in, rubbing his hands together to get some warmth back in them. 'If you're heading toward Plaistow, that would be great.'

'Sure thing,' David said, putting the car into first gear and driving off. 'So, how did you find your first night?'

'Er, yeah. It was fine, thanks, yeah.'

David laughed. 'I bet you hated it. In fact, I'd say you wanted to punch a certain member's lights out? That one you were serving a lot – Mr Measurier, for example?'

'He was a complete arsehole.'

'Don't worry, we've all been there. It goes with the territory, to be honest.'

Tony nodded. 'Do you live near Plaistow?'

'Yeah, Barking. I can drop you off; it's no problem.'

'Thanks for that, David, or can I call you Dave, now

we're out of the confines of the club?'

'Course you can. That's what everybody calls me anyway, apart from inside the club.'

Tony found he had quite a few things in common with Dave, and they relaxed into one another's company, at least until Dave hit Tony with a direct question. 'You're working with Stephen Downer, ain't ya?'

'Er, what?'

Dave laughed. 'It was me who got you that job.'

'Right.'

The car pulled up along Plaistow Broadway. Tony shook Dave's hand and got out. He walked to Rawstone Walk estate with slow, sombre steps, pulling his coat tighter around his body. At least the dismal weather matched his mood.

SERFDOM AND DISORDER

10

February's end was drawing nearer, and although spring approached, the cold weather wouldn't let up. Snow fell in heavy, white clumps. Tony looked out of his kitchen window as if hypnotised by the soft flakes.

'You've held it together in your new job, haven't you?' Veronica said. She sat opposite him, nibbling on a slice of toasted white bread and sipping mouthfuls of tea in-between.

Tony continued to stare out of the window. 'So far, yeah.' He ran his hand through his messed-up hair and scratched under his armpit. His first week had been awful. He hated the surroundings, the club members, and, most of all, his manager, Mr Hayes. He could have done with some answers to his questions, too, but every time he called Stephen, he got his voicemail, and he didn't have the other men's phone numbers. He wanted to know if he had done his 'part' now because he really couldn't see himself lasting much longer.

Veronica pressed against Tony, her warmth seeping into his arm. The silk gown she wore caressed his neck and sent tingles through his body. He smiled as he stroked her thighs. 'I was miles away.' Tony raised her hand to his face and kissed her. 'I've been an asshole of late. I'm sorry.'

She looked into Tony's eyes and leaned forward, brushing her lips against his before pressing closer. He slipped his hands inside her gown and caressed her breasts, squeezing her nipples gently. She kissed him harder and wrapped a leg around his thigh before pulling back with a grin.

'You've had a lot on your mind. You *can* be open with me, though. You do realise that, don't you?'

He tucked a lock of hair behind her ear. 'It's nothing against you. I've just been a little moody this month. You mean everything to me.'

He ran his fingers through her hair, moving in for another kiss. He held her tight, never wanting to let her go.

Tony got himself ready to go out then pulled on his navy-blue woollen hat, thermal gloves, boots, and a goose-down jacket. It looked as if he were ready to go on an expedition to the Arctic Circle.

'I'm going to Uncle Charlie's for a chat and a catch up. Did you want to come?'

Veronica looked up from the chair she had made herself cosy in. 'I think I'll stay here if that's all right with you. Oh, and as you're trying to make things up to me, you can cook a nice Sunday roast when you get back.'

Tony smiled and kissed her on the lips. 'No problem, darling, I've got a nice slice of steak in the fridge. We can have that with some roast potatoes, Yorkshire

SERFDOM AND DISORDER

pudding, and all of the trimmings.'

'I'll peel the potatoes. You can do the rest.'

Tony opened his street door and left the warmth of the flat. He took cautious steps along the icy balcony, his footsteps crunching underfoot as he navigated his way to the stairwell.

The walk to his uncle's house dragged on forever with the snow continuing to fall heavily. Tony scooped his hands to the ground and made a snowball. He glanced around to see if there were any kids to throw it at, but there were none around, so he tossed it at a parked car.

His mind drifted back to when he was a child. All the kids came out to celebrate the white stuff falling, throwing snowballs and making snowmen. It was exciting back then.

Tony reached Uncle Charlie's house and took off his winter accessories, including his snow-covered boots, on his way in. The house was as warm as a sauna, and the smell of Doris's wonderful cooking welcomed him.

'I hear you're working at a gentlemen's club,' said Charlie as he greeted Tony.

'Yeah, I don't know how much longer I'll last, to be honest. It's a nightmare.'

'At least you've got a job. Millions haven't.'

BBC News Twenty-Four glowed out from Charlie's TV screen as a sort of background noise as they chatted.

'Still getting your daily diet of news, Uncle Charlie?'

Charlie grinned and glanced at the TV screen. Five gangland slayings across London the day before was the headline story. It was unusual to hear of so many in one day. Bile burned the back of Tony's throat, and he gagged. The 1066 group's plan was quickly becoming a reality.

'Something big's going to happen, I know these things; I used to be a part of it, remember?'

Tony faced Charlie's gaze. 'I think your imagination's going into overdrive. How would I have any idea about gangland murders? I'm not into that kind of thing.'

Charlie raised his eyebrows, keeping his gaze fixed on Tony.

Tony dangled his keys from his fingertips, half-jumping out of his skin when his mobile rang. It was Stephen Downer. Tony made his excuses and disappeared into the hall to answer the call.

'Tony, its Stephen. Did you hear about the killings in London?'

'Yeah.'

'Can't you talk?'

'No.'

'There's a meeting tonight. The time's come to strike back at Murphy's empire. Seven thirty sharp.'

'Okay, Stephen, I'll see you there,' he said and then ended the call.

Strike at the heart of Murphy's criminal empire? What was he supposed to tell Veronica? He would have to make up another story – and just when he had promised to make things up to her.

'Is there a problem, Tony?'

Tony forced a grin on his face as he sat back down. 'Just meeting up with one of my old pals for a few beers, Uncle Charlie.'

Charlie's eyes narrowed. 'Don't get too boozed up

SERFDOM AND DISORDER

now, will you?'

There was a hint of sarcasm in his voice. Tony fidgeted in his seat. Uncle Charlie was no fool. The longer he stayed, the more chances there were of him getting the truth out of him. He jumped up. 'I should go.'

'You just got here.'

'I know, but I have to get back to Veronica...'

'She's a lovely girl, that one. You should have bought her with you.'

Uncle Charlie waved him away. 'Make sure you say goodbye to Doris on your way out.'

He walked through the kitchen and gave Doris a quick peck on the cheek. 'Sorry, Doris, I know I just got here, but I've got to leave now'

Doris returned to the pastry she was rolling. 'That's okay, love. I'll do you a dinner the next time you're round. Why don't you bring Veronica with you next time? I haven't seen her for a while.'

Tony nodded and left in a hurry. He didn't like the way his uncle kept looking at him. With all the connections Uncle Charlie had made over the years, he could easily find out what was going on, and Tony couldn't risk that. He loved his uncle and didn't want him anywhere near this mess.

He called Stephen on his way home, asking him to ring him at five o'clock that evening. He needed to pretend he was needed at the 1066 club so he could attend the meeting without Veronica getting suspicious.

The afternoon drew to a close. Tony cooked a fantastic roast dinner, and they made the most of their time together. He sat back in the chair, bloated, and burped louder than he'd meant to. Veronica slapped his forearm.

They huddled together on the sofa watching TV when his mobile rang. He glanced at it, feigning surprise as he answered it. 'Hello? Yes, Mr Hayes. Is there a problem?'

He rolled his eyes, and Veronica leaned in close.

'One of our waiters has called in sick. I need you to replace him,' said Stephen in a perfect impression of the well-spoken Mr Hayes. He had never met him but sounded just as authoritative. 'We need you here for seven thirty. We have an important function commencing at eight o'clock sharp.'

'Er... okay, Mr Hayes. I'll be there.'

Tony ended the call with a heavy inhale and a sulky expression. 'Can you believe that? And on a Sunday, too.'

He meant every word, although there was no way around the situation. He had to attend the meeting with Stephen, but it was still a wrench to leave Veronica behind. He tossed the phone onto the sofa.

'I hope they pay well for disrupting your weekend.'

'I'll make sure of it.' Tony gave Veronica a reassuring smile and a wink, and then headed to his bedroom to get changed into his winter clothing again. With the night approaching, the weather would only get worse.

He gave Veronica a tight hug on his way out. 'I'll be back around eleven thirty.'

'You go. I'll be fine. I'm going to raid your DVD collection and watch a few films. You'd better not be home too late, though, I've got a surprise planned for you tonight.'

SERFDOM AND DISORDER

11

It was a terrible night for travelling. The cold bit hard; snow pelted in all directions, limiting Tony's vision. He stopped walking to wipe snow from his face and eyes, yearning for a hot drink. When the office block finally came into view, Tony hurried towards it.

Once inside, he shook the snow off his jacket and stamped his boots up and down, removing an abundance of the frozen white stuff from his feet. The elevator door opened with smooth efficiency and a *ding*, and he entered with slow steps. He pressed the button and took a deep breath as the doors slid closed. The lift took him up to the seventh floor, and he stepped out, walking through the same reception area as before.

He glanced at the wall clock, muttered a curse, and urged his frozen legs to move quicker. As he approached the door he straightened his neck and took another deep breath. Despite committing himself to the fight against the 1066 group and working undercover at the club, besides Stephen, he barely knew the rest of the team. When he reached the door, he paused, taking a moment to gather his thoughts before entering.

J.P. GADSTON

The rest of the team was all present and seated around the table, drinking vending machine tea or coffee from white plastic cups. Like Tony, they were dressed in casual clothes and were deep in conversation. Nobody looked up as he took off his coat, hat, and gloves and slipped silently into the nearest chair. The atmosphere in the room was as welcoming as someone with a social phobia attending a night club.

'Sorry I'm late,' said Tony, glancing at his watch, which read seven thirty-five.

Silence fell across the room. Bob shuffled some papers in front of him, looking as if he were getting ready to talk. Bob looked how Tony imagined an ex-military type to look, with his close-cropped black hair, stocky build, menacing blue eyes, and the SAS emblem tattooed on his forearm, he oozed Special Forces. For a man in his early fifties, Bob looked good in a dark green Fred Perry polo shirt, dark blue jeans, and a pair of rust-coloured Timberland boots.

Tony took the cup of coffee Jim passed him and nodded back in recognition.

Bob cleared his throat. 'Shaun Murphy is attending an amateur boxing event on Thursday at Poplar Town Hall. Our intel says he'll have about ten men with him, each one of them armed.' He glanced around the table. 'We're going to assassinate him. Without Murphy, the No Mercy firm will collapse. But to be on the safe side, we'll take out as many of the firm as possible. Tony, I want you to start a fight in the hall and—'

Tony's stomach lurched. 'Me? Can't someone else do it?' It was bad enough being forced to work in the 1066 club.

SERFDOM AND DISORDER

There was a muffled snigger from John's direction, which was quickly silenced by a glare from Bob. 'I want you and Jim to make it convincing, but not so much that you end up in hospital.'

It looked like he would be in the thick of things, whether he wanted it or not. Tony nodded. 'Shall I put on my boxing headgear before the violence begins?'

Jim slapped Tony on the back. 'You'll need one with me to contend with.'

Bob gave a wry smile and continued. 'Tony and Jim will be close to Murphy. Once the fight begins, the focus will be on you two.'

Richard leaned forward. 'Bob will take Murphy out and make sure it's conspicuous. Once that's done, Simon and I will throw smoke bombs to create a distraction. Bob's going to take as many of the others as he can, too. John will be outside with his car, waiting to get us the hell out of there.'

Tony took a slurp of cheap coffee, getting a few unwanted looks in return. He was impressed with Bob and Richard. Years of experience within the SAS and Royal Marines had given them both a clear insight into how operations were done. They distributed photocopies of the colour-coded seating arrangement at Poplar Town Hall, explained their plan, and then went over it until everyone had a clear understanding of their own role in the operation.

When the meeting finally came to an end, Jim patted Tony on the back. 'How are you enjoying serving the great and the good? I heard you're good friends with Mr Hayes and Mr Measurier now.'

The room broke into laughter. Tony grinned. 'I

wouldn't take the piss too much, Jim. I might hit you harder in our mock fight than you're expecting. Who knows? Maybe Murphy will sign me up to the firm.'

Laughter followed the men as they trailed out of the room, leaving Tony and Stephen on their own. Tony pulled on his warm jacket and woollen hat as he and Stephen headed for the exit together.

On the tube journey home, his mind churned with questions. He glanced at Stephen. 'Your friend, David Ryder, what's his role at the club?'

'He's there for our needs.'

'So, why do you need me when you already have someone inside?'

'We needed you to carry the bugging device.'

Tony's folded his arms and narrowed his eyes. 'What's going on upstairs?'

'That's where the higher-up members discuss business.'

'Why am I barred from working up there?'

'Just focus on your own role.'

Tony sighed. He wanted some reassurance, not more unanswered questions. 'I'm just an ordinary Joe from East London. This is mind-blowing.'

Stephen smiled. 'Dave told me about your constant questioning. You have to trust us, Tony. I understand where you're coming from, but, really, you've got nothing to worry about.'

'If we survive this secret war, you mean? And how am I supposed to get the evening off work?'

Stephen laughed. 'We'll survive; although, Jim packs quite a punch, so who knows? As for the evening off work, we'll arrange it for you, don't worry.'

SERFDOM AND DISORDER

They said their goodbyes at Plaistow station. Stephen turned left, while Tony turned right, heading down the frozen hill. He focused on the icy conditions under his feet, but with his next step, he lost his footing. His heart pounded as he threw out his arms, just managing to grab hold of a streetlight and steady himself. Some kids on the other side of the road laughed and threw snowballs at him. He cursed them, and more snowballs fired in his direction; one splattered on his woollen hat.

Let me get the fuck home and quick. The lure of his warm flat and Veronica quickened Tony's step more than it should have in the slippery conditions, but he managed to keep upright.

As Tony walked along the balcony to his flat, he noticed fresh-looking footprints leading up to and away from his street door. His shoulders stiffened. The door was ajar. He swallowed hard and pushed it open, his heart hammering. Veronica wouldn't have left the door like that, not in this weather or ever.

Tony rushed into the flat and turned on the lights. He ran into the living room first. Her book was resting on the arm of the sofa and her handbag was on the floor, but there was no sign of Veronica. He checked the kitchen next, then the bathroom, before finally throwing the bedroom door open.

He stopped dead.

Veronica was lying on her back on the top of the bed, naked and spread-eagled. Her wrists and ankles were tied to the bed with long lengths of rope. Tears streamed down her face as she cried through the gag in her mouth. A circle of chunky white candles burned around the bed. On the head of the bed, someone had placed a sheet of A4 paper with a message written on it in Old English lettering: '𝔚𝔢 𝔨𝔫𝔬𝔴 𝔶𝔬𝔲𝔯 𝔯𝔬𝔩𝔢; 𝔴𝔢 𝔨𝔫𝔬𝔴 𝔶𝔬𝔲𝔯 𝔣𝔯𝔦𝔢𝔫𝔡𝔰. 𝔜𝔬𝔲 𝔞𝔯𝔢 𝔟𝔢𝔦𝔫𝔤 𝔴𝔞𝔱𝔠𝔥𝔢𝔡. 𝔗𝔥𝔢𝔯𝔢'𝔰 𝔫𝔬 𝔢𝔰𝔠𝔞𝔭𝔢 𝔣𝔯𝔬𝔪 𝔲𝔰.' The message was signed from The Knights of Bayeux.

Tony snapped out of his shock, untied Veronica, and eased the gag from her mouth. She gasped for air as she clung to Tony, her entire body trembling. He wrapped the duvet around her shoulders and held her close. When she was calm enough to release her hold on him, he took Veronica's dressing gown out of the wardrobe and helped her put it on.

He didn't want to risk a fire around the flat and crouched to blow out the candles. When he sat back on the bed, Veronica clutched hold of him again. 'I... I was on the sofa with a glass of wine,' she said in a shaky, high-pitched voice. 'I heard a noise... from the street door, but it sounded like someone walking by, so I ignored it.'

'I feel terrible for not being here.'

'It's not your fault.' Veronica buried herself deeper into his embrace as her tears started again. 'There were three of them. I couldn't see their faces. They wore balaclavas and were dressed all in black, except for the badge—'

'Badge?'

She nodded. 'It was shaped like my school prefect badge, like a shield, I think. It was red and had two golden lions on it.' She sobbed again before continuing. 'They dragged me to the bedroom. I screamed, but no one came. They gagged me, undressed me, and tied me up.'

'They didn't... *hurt* you, did they?'

SERFDOM AND DISORDER

Veronica shook her head. 'No. Nothing like that. Thank God. But I have never been so humiliated. So afraid. They were staring at me, Tony. Speaking – no – chanting in French once all the candles had been lit, and they were making the sign of the cross. They left about thirty minutes ago.'

Tony rummaged through his jacket pocket for his mobile. Instinct told him to call the police, but he was involved in a secret war. Calling them wouldn't be a good idea. He shoved the phone back in his pocket and stood. 'I'll get us a drink. Will you be all right for a minute?'

She nodded and even managed a smile, but she was still visibly shaken. Tony forced himself to remain calm as he walked from the room, resisting the urge to punch the door on his way out. He wanted to hunt down whoever had done this and kill them for what they had put Veronica through.

When he entered the kitchen, he made a quick call to Stephen Downer, describing the scene he had come home to.

'You've got an informant,' he told Stephen. 'It's the only way the 1066 group could have known about my involvement. My money's on David Ryder.'

'Let's not jump to conclusions. Dave might have been interrogated or tortured.'

'And that makes this okay?'

'Of course not. Let me make some calls.'

Tony's face tightened. 'Ring me back in an hour. I want to know who dropped me in it – and why.'

Tony returned to the bedroom with a glass of white wine for Veronica and a beer for himself. Guilt ate at him. He had dragged her into this mess, and she had a right to know what was going on, whether she liked it or not.

After handing Veronica her drink, Tony paced up and down the room, unsure where to start. He wondered if there was any place he could take her to keep her safe. As he turned on his heels, the weird-looking man in the black jumpsuit materialised in front of him.

'Don't be alarmed, Tony, and don't speak aloud. You'll scare Veronica. I can hear your thoughts, remember?'

What do you want now?

'As I've told you before, I'm here to help. It's very difficult getting through to you.'

What?

Lights flashed in front of him. His anger flared as he lost sight of his location. When the intensity faded, he was sitting on Uncle Charlie's sofa. Veronica sat on one side and Doris on the other. Uncle Charlie was in the armchair opposite. 'What the hell?'

Charlie frowned. 'Are you all right, Tony? You look like you've seen a ghost.'

Tony pinched his nose, squeezed his eyes shut, then opened them again. 'Er, yeah, I'm fine. Where was I? My mind's gone blank.'

'You were about to tell us about the 1066 group?'

'Oh, yeah, right...'

He slipped his hand into Veronica's and told them everything he knew about the 1066 group and his involvement so far. At some point through the telling, Veronica had pulled her hand away from his. She looked stunned; they all did.

SERFDOM AND DISORDER

Charlie broke the silence. 'Those gangland murders were carried out by No Mercy, weren't they?'

'Yeah, but there's worse to come.'

Charlie fired questions at him, and Tony did his best to answer them all, but what he really wanted to do was comfort Veronica. She looked devastated, and Tony was afraid this would be too much for her. She had spent her whole life trying to escape the East End. He wouldn't blame her if she wanted to walk away from this, but he hoped she wouldn't. She meant everything to him.

'Can you get in touch with your contacts, Uncle Charlie? Veronica needs somewhere safe to stay – her family, too. I need you on this one.'

'I'll get it arranged.'

Tony nodded his appreciation and turned to Veronica. 'Are you—'

'Just tell me you can find them,' she said, finally looking at him. 'And that you and your friends can stop them.'

He nodded then took her hand into his. 'Everything's going to be fine. We'll get through this mess. Uncle Charlie will make sure of that.'

'Will it be safe to call you?'

'Not for a while. They might trace our calls. We have to be cautious about this; play it safe.'

Veronica's crying resumed. 'What if they get to you? I might never see you again.'

'I'll be fine.'

He bent his head to hers, kissing her hard. He couldn't bear the thought of never seeing her again; just thinking about it was killing him.

Tony's mobile phone rang, and he pulled away from her. It was Stephen. 'I take it you're ready then?'

'Yeah, we'll confront Ryder tonight.'

Tony didn't want to leave Veronica behind – or his aunt and uncle – but duty called. He kissed Veronica goodbye, gave Doris a hug, and shook hands with Charlie.

'Good luck, son. You be careful now,' said Charlie.

Tony nodded and stepped into the night. He had a strong yearning to see David Ryder and find out if he was responsible for Veronica's ordeal.

SERFDOM AND DISORDER

12

The snowfall was just as bad in Barking as elsewhere, shining brightly against the dimly lit streets leading up to David's house. The place was a stereotypical suburban street: dull, unimaginative, and uniform. Too many houses in too small an area.

Tony and Stephen parked on the street and headed to David's door. 'What shall we do, break in or knock?' Tony asked in hushed tones.

'Knock first. We don't want to arouse suspicion, do we?'

Tony resisted the urge to boot David's door off its hinges. He stooped beside the grey wheelie bin and picked up a loose brick.

'What are you doing?' Stephen hissed.

Tony glared at him. 'I've had enough of being Mister Nice Guy. He could have gotten Veronica killed.'

Stephen gripped Tony's hand and forced it downward. The brick loosened in his hand and fell to the floor. 'Look, Tony, we don't want to get arrested. Keep a clear head. We'll knock on the door, and we'll see what he's got to say.'

Stephen rang the doorbell. Tony speculated whether Ryder would open the door or not. *That traitorous bastard had better get out of bed and come down here.*

Minutes passed without an answer. Tony glanced at the wheelie bin, contemplating throwing it through the living room window, but the door opened and a head popped around it. Ryder's face turned ashen at the sight of Tony and Stephen.

Unable to contain his emotions any longer, Tony booted the door. He didn't have time for diplomacy. Ryder stumbled against the wall, lost his balance, and fell to the floor. Tony and Stephen rushed inside, shutting the door behind them. They dragged Ryder into the living room and threw him into an armchair.

Ryder's mouth froze open, but no words came out. His wife called down from upstairs, wanting to know what was going on, and his little girl was crying in the background.

Tony backed away from him. 'Go upstairs and reassure your wife and child that everything's okay, then get back down here. We need to talk. And don't bother telling her who we are. It'll make things worse for you.'

Ryder wrung his hands as he nodded. His eyes were bulbous, and he seemed on the verge of having a heart attack, never once asking what they were doing at his house; it seemed he understood the reason for their visit.

Stephen glowered at Tony and stepped towards Ryder. 'We just want to ask you a few questions. We won't harm you.'

Ryder disappeared and returned a few minutes later. The ashen complexion had faded, and he slumped in his armchair in what looked like resignation.

'You know why we're here, don't you?' Tony asked.

'They threatened my wife and kid... I had to tell them.'

Tony took off his woolly hat and stared at Ryder.

'What happened?' Stephen asked.

Ryder's face sagged. 'Friday, I got summoned to Mr Hayes' office. He poured me a cup of tea, we had a chat, and I came over all drowsy. When I came around, I was tied to a chair and surrounded by a bunch of men in balaclavas – called themselves the Knights of Bayeux.'

Tony glanced at Stephen, exchanging a look with him. 'Who are these Knights?'

Stephen shrugged and stared back at Ryder. 'Anything else you can tell us?'

'I'd heard rumours about their existence, but I thought it was a load of nonsense. Most of the gossip was about them being ex-Special Forces, or something. They do the dirty work for their pay masters or, if you like, mercenaries. They make sure no one interferes with 1066 business. Turns out they were watching me.' He looked at Tony. 'And when you turned up on my reference, they got suspicious. Yes, I told them about your role at the club. My wife and kid were being threatened. What was I supposed to do?'

Stephen sighed. 'Don't worry. We won't hurt you.'

Tony walked up to Stephen and whispered in his ear, 'My Uncle Charlie has contacts. He's putting Veronica, my aunty Doris, and himself someplace safe. I think we should do the same for all our families – including Ryder's – don't you?'

Stephen nodded approvingly then patted Ryder on

the shoulder. 'We'll get someone to relocate you and your family. You know too much. I'm puzzled why they didn't kill you during the interrogation.'

Ryder settled into a more comfortable position, breathing out a long sigh of relief. 'Apart from you and Stephen, Tony's the only person I know in your group. I hope I haven't ruined too much.'

Tony whispered into Stephen's ear. 'We'll have to cancel the mission, you realise that?'

Stephen's head dropped a touch as he whispered, 'Yeah.'

Tony patted Ryder on the shoulder. 'What else do these Knights have on us?'

'They already suspect that there's a movement getting ready to stop the 1066 group. I don't know how much they know, though. Maybe they're watching everyone in your group. I'm speculating, but you never know with these people. They're professional in how they monitor things and get information. The Knights of Bayeux trust no-one but their club members, and their fellow Knights, of course.'

Stephen's face flushed. He took his mobile out of his pocket. 'I hope we're not the only two left.' He tapped his phone's touch screen and put it to his ear. His teeth clenched as he waited. 'Come on, come on, answer the fucking phone!'

Three out of the five other men answered his call. He outlined what had happened and the consequences their movement faced. It was agreed they would rendezvous at eight on Monday, provided Stephen could get in touch with the other two. There was no mention about evacuating their families.

Tony phoned Uncle Charlie and asked him to send someone to collect Ryder and his family. They needed to be somewhere safe until they could find a more permanent safe house for their families.

Within forty minutes of Tony calling Charlie, a car arrived for Ryder and his distraught family to take them to a destination Stephen and Tony knew nothing about. It had to be that way, in case they were captured and tortured.

The driver of the car, a good friend of Charlie's called Ray Jennings, gripped Tony's arm. 'Don't worry. Everyone's in good hands. There's no way anyone will find them.' He leaned forward, putting his lips to Tony's ears. 'Your uncle's armed to the teeth. We've got some of Charlie's old pals with us, too. Everyone's in good company.'

Ray shook Tony's hand, winked at him, and walked around to the driver's side of the car. As the car departed, Tony smiled. It was reassuring to know his family and Ryder's were in safe hands.

13

The meeting took place deep in a small beer cellar with a low ceiling in a pub in Aldgate. Tony brushed away the cobwebs sticking to his hair and dust from his jacket. Stephen had eventually managed get in contact with the other two men, so they were all present. Simon was a friend of the landlord and had arranged for them to have a safe place for a meeting. Some heated exchanges passed between them as they sat on stainless steel beer kegs with their backs bent forward and their shoulders hunched, debating what to do next. Tony kept his mouth covered with his hands, owing to the persistent bouts of coughing brought on by the dusty cellar.

Even though there was beer all around them, they abstained from drinking. They discussed the cancellation of Murphy's execution at Poplar town hall with angry, resentful tones, then proceeded to talk about other important matters.

After listening to the exchange of views, Tony made a point nobody else had raised. 'If the 1066 group have been tailing us, wouldn't they have executed us by now?

SERFDOM AND DISORDER

Or tried to? It seems odd they haven't.'

Bob nodded. 'I agree. Something doesn't seem right. Perhaps it was just a scare tactic?' He glanced around. 'Still, the obvious target is the 1066 group, and I have a plan for that, but let's keep focused on Murphy. Let's find a way of hurting him first, shall we?'

They reached the same agreement. Murphy had to be contained – and soon. Once the East End gangster's power was diminished, the 1066 group would have to find someone else to do their dirty work. During that time, it would enable them to then turn on the instigators of the situation: the 1066 group itself.

Bob's eyes narrowed. 'I've had people doing surveillance. We'll hit Murphy where it hurts – his wallet. He has a few brothels in Soho. They're open twenty-four hours a day, and we'll hit two of them. Tomorrow. Are there any dissenters?'

No one disagreed, so Bob opened a large, black sports bag and handed out photographs of the two brothels. Dirty exterior walls with fading white paint and black doors that needed a coat of gloss paint. Rubbish of every description littered the entrance.

Bob lifted his bag onto the table and encouraged everyone to look inside. 'Uzi machine guns and Beretta 92 S handguns. A pair for each of us. We can't afford to leave anything to chance.'

Tony recoiled from the bag, his mouth and eyes opened wide. The realisation of what he had got involved in hit him like a punch in the face. 'Fucking hell, Bob, how did you get hold of these – or shouldn't I ask?'

'We can't arrive at a gangster's brothel with baseball

bats, can we? As for where I got the arms from, you're right. You shouldn't ask.'

Each of the men took their weapons and eyed them up and down. Tony picked up an Uzi, feeling like a kid about to play some war games. He held the machine gun and imagined firing off a few rounds.

Bob grinned and wiped his forehead. 'We'll split into two groups. Tony and Jim will be with me. The rest of you can band together with Richard. Right, put the guns back in the bag.' Bob winked at Richard and frowned at the others. 'I've arranged a trip to a shooting range to get you rookies some practice. The manager's an ex-pal from yester-year, so we'll have the range to ourselves. I paid enough dosh to secure the hire of the place, so make sure you fucking listen to what I have to say. I want the raid to happen tomorrow. We don't want to leave things too long.

'We're going to raid the safes in these brothels. I'll show Richard how to crack open a safe without explosives. I've got a couple of safes being delivered to the gun range, too, so we can have a practice run.'

The team drove to a shooting range in the Hertfordshire countryside, on the outer perimeter of North London. It was situated around the back of a large country house – a long, narrow room of grey concrete slabs and hard, stone flooring. At one end of the room, there were four tables sectioned off to place weapons on. The other end of the room had four circular targets made from thick paper that hung from clips attached to the ceiling. Black and white stripes decorated the targets around the circumference with a small red circle in the middle. On normal occasions, the range was

SERFDOM AND DISORDER

reserved for members.

Bob placed some ear defenders on the tables, and each of the men grabbed a pair and placed them around their necks. Next, he pulled an Uzi out of the large sports bag. 'Right, you horrible bleeders, this is how it's done. Pull out the stock at the bottom of the weapon and place it against your shoulder, which gives you a steadier shot. Load your magazine and place it into the magazine well.'

Bob smacked the magazine hard into the well, and it clicked. 'It's always best to hit the magazine hard, just to be sure it's loaded.' He showed them where the two safety levers were to make sure the gun didn't go off accidently, and he pulled a latch back at the top of the weapon. It clicked back and released the safety.

Bob set the weapon to pistol so single shots would ring out. 'Okay, we're on pistol setting. If we run into trouble, we can set it to machine gun, which I'm sure you're aware will blast out more bullets per second. Place the stock on your shoulder, grip one hand under the barrel, and the other hand around the magazine with your finger over the trigger. Put your cheek down onto the site, and you're ready to fire.'

He placed the ear defenders around his head, and a round of single shots rang out from the Uzi, each one hitting its target. Bob then put the Uzi into machine gun mode and rang out a rapid succession of accurate shots.

Bob pointed to Tony, Jim, Stephen, and Simon: 'Right, I want you four tossers to go up to the table and fire at the targets, and be careful. Make sure you know where the safety levers are.'

J.P. GADSTON

Tony put the ear defenders on. Butterflies fluttered in his stomach. Following Bob's lead, he fired off a volley of single shots at the designated target. The stock impacted into his shoulder, and he jerked back a little. His shots went a little wide of the target. He grimaced. *This is gonna be a long day.*

After four hours of practice, they all had a good idea of how to handle their designated weapons. They were no experts, but in close combat, with an Uzi set to machine gun mode, a rapid spray of bullets had to hit something.

'Okay, I've bored you to death with shooting and how to handle a weapon. I'm going to show Richard a simple but effective method of how to break a safe open now.'

Bob ushered them out of the shooting range and along a short corridor into another room where five safes were spread out around an otherwise empty area. They looked ancient, with rusting on their sides and paint peeling off, but looked otherwise secure. On the floor were a hammer and a small and long crow bar.

'Right, Rich, this is basic. It can be done in two to three minutes.'

Bob handed Simon his phone. 'There's a stopwatch on there. I want you to time this, so you can all see that it's achievable in the time I stated.'

Bob hammered away at a furious pace, and metallic clangs echoed around the room. A small bead of sweat trickled down Bob's face, but he made the job look easy.

Simon stopped the time. 'Two minutes and ten seconds.'

Bob waved his arm. 'Okay, Rich, it's your turn now,

mate.'

Richard worked through the safes with back-breaking aplomb. The hammer and crowbars smashed through the job with a barrage of clangs. Richard reached an acceptable level of safe cracking competence and received a round of applause from everyone present. He wiped the sweat from his forehead and bowed. 'That's knocked the crap out of me. My arms are killing me.'

Bob grinned. 'Now we're ready.'

14

The next morning, Bob gathered them together at an old empty office space in Moorgate. A scowl crossed his face. 'I know none of you, apart from Richard, have faced a situation like this before, and you're no doubt daunted by it all, but there's no other way. We've got two vans waiting for us around the corner. Let's get out and show this Murphy bastard what we're about.'

There were nods of agreement all round; each man seemed ready for what lay ahead. They had to be. There was no running away now.

'My group will go to the brothel at the back of Brewer Street,' Bob continued. 'The other group will hit Berwick Street. I've booked two parking spots at Brewer Street NCP, so we don't have to waste time driving around looking for a parking spot. When you get to the brothel, pretend you're punters and make it sound genuine. There'll be armed doormen inside. Shoot them. I've fitted silencers on our weapons, so gunfire won't draw attention. This isn't target practice. You'll be at close quarters. We don't want to leave Murphy's security lying around.

SERFDOM AND DISORDER

'Once the doormen are taken out, head upstairs and get the prostitutes and punters out of their rooms. There'll be armed men upstairs too. Take them out. The safe is in the office.'

Simon shook his head. 'What are we supposed to do with the prostitutes and their punters? We can't just leave them there, can we? Once we've got the money, there's the brothel itself. Do we burn the place down so Murphy's money earner goes with it?

'Yeah, burn it down. As for the prostitutes and punters, I've got that covered. We'll put them in the vans and dump them in a field in Berkshire.'

Simon had a blank look: 'Why Berkshire? And why a field?"

'Because it's out of the way. It's not drawing attention to us, and it isn't too far from London. Anything else for fuck sake?'

Tony was relieved to be in Bob's team. The raid would be a piece of piss for an ex-SAS veteran.

The men shook each other's hands and stepped towards their allotted vehicles. Tony gave the other team a thumbs up. 'Good luck, lads.'

Bob maneuvered the London traffic with an ease that came from years of experience of battling the busy streets. They reached Brewer Street and entered the multi-storey car park. Tony frowned. It would be his first time firing a weapon at a human target, and he wasn't entirely sure he could do it – if it even came to that. Maybe the threat of carrying a weapon would be enough?

The brothel's entrance was tucked away down a narrow back road. It was dirty and cold, and there was litter everywhere – an appropriate setting for one of Murphy's illicit enterprises.

'There's CCTV outside the door. I need to hack into the system before we go in,' said Bob.

Jim smiled. 'How do you know so much about this place, Bob? You're not a regular are you?'

Bob laughed and shook his head. 'Trust you to come out with a gag like that just before a shooting spree, but no, it's had a stakeout, same as the other targets.' He passed the small canister of petrol he was carrying to Tony. 'Hold onto that. We'll need it when we've finished our other business.'

Tony wiped sweat from his brow. During the meeting in the pub cellar, he'd felt bold at the thought of raiding the brothel, but reality was biting now. Things were different. Bob gave him an uneasy look and a raised eyebrow.

About forty feet away from the entrance, Bob raised his hand for them to stop. 'Stand over there with your backs to the wall.'

Bob pulled a handheld IP scanner out of his pocket, readying it to hack the CCTV system. Tony watched Bob weave his magic, both fascinated and shocked at how easy he made hacking look.

'Right, lads, we're in. The CCTV's down,' Bob said after only a couple of minutes. He put the scanner away and led them to the entrance: a solid black, windowless door. Tony glanced over his shoulder to see if anyone was behind them and was reassured to see there wasn't.

Bob placed his finger on the buzzer. There was a long wait, or so it seemed. In reality, it lasted about thirty seconds. Tony spat on the dirt below him as his throat congested.

When the door shrieked open, a mountain of a man with slicked, black hair stood before them. His suit bulged with muscle, and he wielded a baseball bat. He didn't look like a bloke to mess with. The doorman's eyes widened, and he grunted like a pig as he attempted to shut the door. Bob's reactions were quicker. A few shots from the silenced Berretta impacted the doorman's chest. He fell to the ground with a thud.

They stepped over the body and entered the brothel, creeping up the narrow staircase that would lead them to where the real action took place.

Tony gripped his pistol tighter. Bile rose into his throat and hit his taste buds. Loud, electronic music drifted towards them, along with the sound of men and women laughing.

At the top of the stairs was a wall to the right and a small corridor to the left, at the bottom of which stood a painted blue door. Two men, dressed in suits, stood outside. Bob fired another couple of shots before they had taken a single step forward. They slumped to the floor, blood seeping from their heads.

Bob turned to Tony and Jim. 'Are you ready for this?'

Before either of them could answer, Bob booted the door open. The two men followed him inside. It was like something from a futuristic orgy. The room was dark apart from disco lights, a laser, and a dry ice machine. The music had a heavy electronic influence, its deep beat shook the speakers. There were naked women everywhere – at least ten of them – and five men aged from their early fifties to sixties. Each of the men were in a state of undress; shirts, ties, trousers and underpants were scattered around the room.

Prostitutes performed different favours to satisfy their clients' needs. Screams and moans blended with the thumping music. The aromatic smell of cannabis drifted around the room with lines of cocaine prepared on the glass tables and a variety of booze.

Tony's eyes widened. An odd sensation swept through him as he studied the scene before him. It was like watching the event through someone else's eyes, almost like an out-of-body experience. His stance slumped a little. Reality drifted back when he recognised two of the men as politicians he'd seen on TV.

All at once, the scene collapsed into chaos. The prostitutes screamed and grabbed for clothing, sounding like a band of wailing banshees. The one closest to them clutched a shirt to her chest. 'We'll do anything you want. Just don't kill us.'

The men attempted to cover themselves up, too. One of the clients covered his private parts with a trembling hand. 'If it's money you're after, take what you want. Just let me leave here in one piece.'

Bob waved his pistol around and pointed it at the knee-high coffee table. 'All of you, throw your phones on the table. If any of you try any nonsense, we'll shoot you.'

Prostitutes and clients alike searched for their phones. Tony kept alert. Within half a minute, there was a mass of phones on the table.

Jim looked around and grabbed a small bin from the corner of the room and swept the phones into it.

Tony grinned as he tugged Bob's coat and whispered, 'I think we got lucky here. You know who these men are, don't you?' Bob shook his head, and Tony's grin grew. 'They're cabinet members. What do you think the odds are that the other three work at the Home Office?'

Bob chuckled. The music still boomed, and Tony fired into each of the speakers. Glowing embers sparked as the sound came to an abrupt halt, but the strobe lights persisted with its annoying flickering. Tony turned on the main lights to search for the power source. When he found it, he flicked the switch and the lightshow ended.

'Is there anyone in the office?' Bob asked the woman nearest to him. 'And you'd better not lie.'

'The manager.'

Bob scowled at the door.

One of the women flicked her hair back. 'It's soundproof. The bloke in there can't hear a thing. Just sits and watches TV.'

Bob nodded to Tony. 'Keep an eye on this lot. If anyone does something stupid, shoot them. Oh, and can all of you hurry up and get dressed? If I think someone's attempting to hold us up, I'll be sending a bullet your way.'

Bob ordered Jim to get the van ready for the getaway. 'The coordinates for where I want you to drive are in the dash.'

Jim nodded and turned to walk out of the room, placing the bin filled with phones in the corner of the room. He stopped and glared at one of the half-naked men for a moment, as if he, too, recognised him.

Bob approached the manager's door. He tried the door handle. It rattled but wouldn't open. He gestured to one of the women. 'Get your fucking manager on the intercom.'

She hurried to the door and did as he asked. 'Eddie, its Kelly. A punter's in a bad way. You need to get out here and fast.'

When the door unlocked, Bob shoved it open, knocking the manager backwards. As he stepped inside, he raised his gun arm. Two dull thuds came from the room.

Tony stepped back, keeping his gun pointed at everyone as he glanced over his shoulder to see if Bob was okay. The manager was slumped on the floor – lifeless. A strong smell of cannabis drifted from the office; a joint was burning in the manager's ashtray.

Bob took two crowbars and a hammer out of the black sports bag and set to work opening the safe.

Tony waved his pistol around, demanding quiet as the sound of metal impacting metal rang out. He took another quick peek and saw Bob smashing the crow bar with the hammer. Bob's face was contorted in concentration and determination.

The hammering came to a stop, and when he looked again, Bob had the door open and was taking wads of money from the safe. He was in awe of how much money was in the safe. There had to be at least fifty grand in notes.

Bob emerged from the office looking more menacing than ever now he was in SAS mode. He glanced at Tony. 'Pass me that petrol canister.'

Bob took the canister and poured petrol around the office. He pulled out a matchbox and struck a match, throwing it on the carpet and watching the flames spread through the office.

Tony waved his gun in the air. 'Let's get you lot out of here. Any funny business, and I won't hesitate to shoot.'

They hurried out of the room and down the stairs, their expressions betraying their fear. Much to Tony's relief, nothing happened.

As they emerged in the road, a figure caught the corner of Tony's eye. The man in the black jumpsuit, leaning against the wall.

What do you want?

'Just watching. Keep up the good work.' He disappeared in the blink of an eye.

The women huddled together shivering, while their clients stood in single file outside the entrance. None of them uttered a word.

Bob came to the front and turned to face them. 'Come on, get moving. Any slacking and I'll shoot the lot of you.'

The prisoners had ashen faces, trembling lips and chins, and tight shoulders as they marched to the back of the van Jim had reversed into the narrow road. Bob and Tony sat in the back with them, pointing weapons in their direction. Jim slammed the back door shut and locked it. A couple of the women were crying, and one of the men looked close to tears. The rest of them sat silently, either in shock or lost in thought. Tony glared at the men without remorse. The shit would hit the fan now. This was a full-on war with no turning back.

The prisoners remained quiet on the journey out of London. One woman offered Tony money to secure their freedom.

'Put your fucking money away. I'm not for sale.'

Bob leaned forward, his arm raised as if to pistol whip her. Tony held his arm back.

'Count your lucky stars this bloke stopped me,' Bob snarled.

Bob's mobile phone rang. 'How did your mission go?' He listened and then glanced at Tony. 'Everything's worked out just right. No causalities. There were some officials there, too.' He winked. 'Yes, take them as prisoners,' he said into the phone. 'They'll prove valuable for us.'

They stopped driving after around forty minutes, the last ten of which had been on bumpy back roads. When the van stopped, Jim unlocked the backdoor, revealing a rural setting – a field in Berkshire. Bob pointed his Uzi towards the door. 'Right, ladies, you can fuck off back to London and continue to suck cock.'

'Why aren't we being released?' one of the men – a politician – asked, his face all flustered.

Bob turned to face him. 'Keep your fucking mouth shut, or I'll put a bullet in it.'

Tony climbed out after the women and slammed the door shut. The other team's van was parked beside them. They had some prostitutes to off-load, too.

Richard walked over to Tony and blew out a heavy sigh. 'Glad you're all okay.'

Tony nodded. He was just as relieved as Richard was.

Bob pointed to an opening in the field. 'That's the way out. Turn left and keep walking. There's a station's about fifteen minutes away. Now piss off.'

The women hugged each other; although, one or

SERFDOM AND DISORDER

two groaned at the news they would have to make the journey home on their own.

Once the women were far enough away, Bob glanced at Tony. 'I want you in the back of the van with me. We going to have a little chat with our prisoners.' He placed the palm of his hand on his shaved head and closed his eyes as if lost in thought. He mumbled to himself before addressing Jim. 'I want to drive somewhere. I'll tell you where to go in a moment.'

Bob and Tony climbed into the back of the van. The prisoners cried out for mercy, and one of them clutched onto Bob's trouser leg. His face was pale, and he stammered when he spoke. 'W-what do you want from us? We haven't harmed you in any way. W-what's the problem?'

Bob narrowed his eyes and grimaced. 'We want to know about your plans to turn Britain into a nation of servitude and misery. We want information about Shaun Murphy, and we want a full timetable of the events you've got planned.' He paused. 'If you don't answer our questions, the pain you'll experience will be so bad, you'll beg to tell us everything.' His scowl deepened. 'There's no turning back from here, gentlemen.'

Bob and Tony left the van and locked the door. Bob's nostrils flared as he turned and looked at Richard. 'We're taking these bastards to an empty warehouse in Slough. It's a twenty-minute drive from here.'

'We'll follow you,' Richard said.

Bob patted Richard on the back. 'Yeah, no problem, Rich. You've done good work today; we all have.

Tony raised his thumb at Bob. 'I dread to think what

you have in store for them.'

'Let's just say I have ways of getting information when it's needed.'

Bob handed Jim a slip of paper. 'Here are the directions to the warehouse. Me and Tony will be in the back of the van with the prisoners. The other van will be following, so don't lose them.'

Jim stared at the directions. 'It shouldn't be a problem.'

Bob rubbed his hands together. 'Let's get this show on the road, then.'

15

Jim found the warehouse in Slough easily enough, and the other van followed behind with no setbacks. Bob and Tony got out of their van, locking the backdoor as they did so. Bob unlocked the industrial sliding door, and the vans reversed inside the warehouse before Bob slid the door to a close.

They ordered the officials out of the vans and led them to a set of old chairs in the centre of the empty warehouse.

Bob nodded to the back of the open van. 'Tony, there's a navy-blue canvas bag in the back. Can you bring it along?'

Tony did as he was asked and wondered what was inside. He knew it would be inappropriate to peek inside.

The nine men sat in a line. Their hands were bound to the chairs and pinned behind their backs; pillow cases had been pulled over their heads. They trembled with fear. One man had urinated on himself, and another was crying.

'You can't do this to us,' one of the bolder men cried out. 'Are you aware of who we are?'

Bob scratched his bollocks. 'There's no need to panic. Just tell us what we want to hear, and you'll be back home in bed playing happy families with the wife.'

Tony couldn't hazard a guess of what Bob's next move would be. He was a passenger on a ride orchestrated by Bob Davis. Out of all of them, Bob was the only one with any interrogation training.

'It's in your interest to cooperate; otherwise, your chance of seeing freedom will be slim, and… you'll be in a lot of pain. It's simple. Comply and you'll be fine.'

The men spoke at once, begging for mercy. They seemed ripe to reveal everything Bob wanted to hear. They were pampered public school boys, ignorant about want and struggle, and had no regard for people like himself. Tony had a certain sympathy for them. A jolt made his left thigh twitch, and he slapped it. Richard and Stephen glanced at him with puzzled looks.

Bob gestured to Tony. 'Take the hoods off their heads.'

Nausea overwhelmed Tony. He coughed, drawing perplexed eyes from the rest of his team. As he approached the chairs, the man closest to him mumbled a prayer; the others breathed heavily. Tony reminded himself who these people were and their role behind Murphy's activities. His discomfort subsided a little. He pulled off the hoods, and the men grimaced.

Bob grabbed the navy-blue canvas bag and dumped it on the floor before the prisoners with an almighty thud. A cloud of dust rose from the dirty concrete floor. The prisoners jerked upright. Some wrestled with the bindings around their wrists and ankles. Bob glared at the hostages and unzipped the bag. He reached inside and withdrew a cordless drill. He revved it and glanced along the line. 'It's no good you bastards crying now, is it? What will happen next is that I'll ask you a question and I expect to receive an answer. If that answer is what I want to hear, then I'll be lenient with you. If it's not, you'll feel the full force of my drill in your kneecaps.'

The prisoners rocked to and fro in their chairs, trying desperately to break free. It was disturbing to see men reduced to nothing, and made worse by Bob as he continued to rev the drill.

Bob turned to Tony. 'Can you get me a black leather strap from the bag?'

'What's that for?'

'Whoever doesn't give me the correct answer before I drill.'

Tony handed the strap to Bob, who turned and pointed to a prisoner. 'You first. You're aware of the consequences if you don't comply, aren't you?'

The man shook his head and whimpered. Bob grinned and continued to rev the drill. He seemed to get a thrill out of watching the man squirm.

'Your name please, sir.'

'G-G-Giles Ca-a-ampbell.'

'Okay, Giles, I want you to tell me who you work for and if you have a role within the 1066 group.'

Campbell opened his mouth, but no words came out. Bob produced a bottle of water from the outside of his jacket pocket. He gave Campbell a few mouthfuls.

Bob stepped away from his prisoner and approached his team. He gestured for them to come closer then whispered, 'Think I went over the top a bit there. I'll let things cool down for five minutes and then give him more water. By then, he should be able to talk.'

The minutes dragged by in silence. Bob walked up to Campbell and gave him the water before producing the drill again and revving it up. He waved it near to Campbell's knees.

Campbell grimaced and shut his eyes.

'Do you want your fucking kneecaps?' Bob shouted over the noise. 'Who are you, what's your connection to the 1066 group, and what do you know about Murphy?'

'I-I am a senior official at the Home Office. I helped the group with their plans. W-We are using Shaun Murphy to control the criminal underworld.'

'Now tell me something I don't know.'

'He gets help from the Knights of Bayeux. They help Murphy's henchmen assassinate key criminals up and down the country, but he is nothing more than our puppet. He serves our purposes. We don't serve his.'

'What about the police? Why are they involved in this?'

Campbell's eyes shifted, and his mouth shook a little. 'There's a hell of a lot of resentment within the police force. They have pandered to criminals for far too long. We're using their resentment and Shaun Murphy's lust for power to manipulate the situation to suit our requirements.'

'Anarchy, you mean?'

'The 1066 group will lobby the political elite at Westminster, and they will get what they want: a totalitarian state.'

'But what does the 1066 group get out of it?'

'Power and profit. The plan is to put everyone, apart

SERFDOM AND DISORDER

from the higher members of society, into a prison-like system. They will be placed into a purpose-built camp. They'll receive no pay but be provided with food, clothing, and a roof. Each person will receive a role from the state, which they will play within society. If the individual refuses, they will face a firing squad.'

'Allotted role, like what?'

'They will be assessed for their strengths and weaknesses and given a role that best suits their skill. Not only that, but they're expected to work twelve hours a day, seven days a week. There will be a quota of work expected of them, and they will have to report back to their sleeping quarters. The camps shall get built everywhere.'

'What about the houses people are living in now? What happens to them?'

'Reminders of decadent times. A reminder of the lives people once had that will never return.'

'So, the 1066 group will lead Britain back to the days of serfdom, a society based on Norman principles? A society where most of the nation's people will live a life of hell?'

'Yes, and anyone who questions their new lives or complains in any form will receive the hangman's noose or a firing squad'

Tony pulled Bob aside and whispered into his ear. 'Why are you asking questions we already know the answers to?'

'Just part of the process.'

Bob glared at the captives and put the drill back in his bag. 'That's it for now. There will be more questions, somewhere down the line.' He glanced at Jim. 'Can you get the van over here? We'll load the prisoners inside.'

The van reversed towards the captives. Bob opened the back door. Each prisoner was untied and put in the back of the van. Jim nodded towards Bob. He slammed the door shut, jumped in the driver's seat, and drove off.

Bob sported a sarcastic smile on his face. 'Come on, then. I think we'd better head off to a safe place and plan our next move. We've got to get at Murphy and destroy the 1066 group. Not much of a tall order, is it?'

Everyone laughed as they climbed into the second van and drove on.

SERFDOM AND DISORDER

16

Bob had chosen a hideout deep in the New Forest, within the county of Hampshire: a large wooden cabin that could sustain the group easily. It was built as a hideaway for senior officials during the early nineteen seventies, in preparation for a potential invasion from the forces of the Warsaw Pact during the Cold War. Once the Cold War had ended, the hut was abandoned by the Ministry of Defence. It was still in pristine condition.

After driving through the dirt track lanes deep into the Forest, they arrived at their destination. Tony stared at the hut and gasped. He suspected Bob had been here before and perhaps lived there for a time. *Somebody* had maintained it. It had a tiled roof, a beautiful grassland border, and a distinctive wooden fence. There were glass windows to the left and right of the front entrance door. The wood on the exterior looked as if it had been treated with a preservative. It looked welcoming.

Tony patted Bob on the back. 'Blimey, Bob, this is lovely. I bet it's a joy to be here when the weather's nice.'

'Yeah, sometimes it's difficult to leave and go back

home. It's a great place to relax – or hide.'

The front door of the cabin was like any other: white, heavy-duty plastic with a frosted glass window at the top. Bob opened the door, and everyone entered with their luggage. Tony felt safe for the first time in ages, although it was just as cold inside the cabin as out. He glanced at the fireplace and wondered how cosy it would be once the fire was going.

'Tony,' said Bob, 'if you go out the back door and into the shed, you'll find a stack of chopped logs. Here… take the key.'

Tony went and fetched the wood. Once the fire was lit, the warmth felt glorious. Tony sat in front of it, staring into the crackling flames.

'There's no chance of the heat escaping,' Bob said. 'There's insulation in the walls and ceiling. It'll be so hot in here soon; you'll all be taking your jackets and jumpers off.'

The cabin had an open-floor plan. Sleeping bags waited for them on top of single mattresses. There was a large wooden dining table and a cooker that ran on gas canisters on the other side of the room. Electricity came from the generator outside, and running water came from a well with a pump to pull the water to the surface. There was a water heater, too, and outside, there was a stand-alone toilet in a small hut. The set-up was basic, but it was a great place to hide away and plan their next move.

Everyone stood in awe at what Bob had created – the perfect rural retreat. Tony basked in the tranquility of it all, but he had a question that wouldn't go away. "How did you get hold of this hut Bob, are you a squatter or something?'

He grinned. 'It's mine because I told the Ministry of Defence a group of international bird watchers were going to claim it. It's amazing what you can achieve with a fake letterhead. I received a response a few weeks later saying the cabin was mine. I think they were glad to get rid of it.'

Bob turned the gas cooker on and took food out of one of the many bags to prepare their meal. It wasn't anything too exotic, just standard British fare: mince beef pie, mashed potatoes, vegetables, and beef gravy. He turned out to be handy at cooking. The pie was huge, delicious, and big enough to feed everyone gathered. The golden pastry topping filled the cabin with a delicious, home-cooked smell. Tony's mouth quivered in anticipation. He sat at the table and picked up his cutlery, tapping them on his hands.

Once the meal was served, no one needed any prompting to eat. They shovelled the food into their mouths, as if it were the first meal anyone had eaten in a week.

Richard stared at Bob. 'So where are the prisoners being held?'

'Safe house in north-west London.'

As soon as they had finished eating, the drinking began. Bob had thought to bring ten cases of lager as part of their provisions. Tony poured lager down his throat and let off continual rounds of burps in-between. He felt like an Old English king at a banquet. His stomach felt close to exploding, and the others confessed to feeling the same. Glazed eyes, red faces, and wide smiles gleamed as they as they leaned back on some heavy beanbags around the fireplace.

Simon glanced at Tony. 'You realise you're dragging the tone down, don't you?'

'What do you mean?'

'You're like a British tourist on holiday with your constant burping, you uncouth bastard.'

Everyone roared with laughter, pointing a finger at Tony and giving him some friendly abuse. They drank into the night. It appeared they all wanted to get drunk.

Tony's gaze fixed on the fire. He wanted to enjoy the moment while it lasted, but his vision distorted and the tunnel of golden light appeared. 'We're back in communication. Can you hear me, Tony?'

Who are you? I keep asking and never get a response. Am I going insane or what?

'You're not going insane. We represent your best interests because you're important to us.'

The tunnel disappeared, leaving Tony feeling as confused as all the other times it had happened. The experience depressed him more than anything else. His face sagged, and he stared harder into the flames. He broke his focus with quick gulps of lager. He didn't involve himself in any more of the drunken antics; although, the other men's laughter and name calling carried on. Tony's mind drifted from them.

John tugged at Tony's arm. 'Are you okay, Tony? You look like you're in another dimension.'

Tony glanced around the room. 'Does David know what's going on upstairs in the 1066 club?'

Silence. He glanced around again, then threw his empty beer can into the fire.

Richard straightened with some effort and grimaced.

SERFDOM AND DISORDER

'We know what's going on upstairs, but I don't think you're ready to hear it just yet.'

Tony stood. The room spun, and he put his hand on the wall to steady himself. 'I've had enough of you fuckers keeping information from me. Am I a part of this team or what?'

Richard glanced at the others, who looked back at him with stern faces. All signs of their earlier merriment had gone.

'Okay, Tony, but what you're about to hear might unsettle you.'

Tony didn't know whether to laugh or cry at the anticipation. The fire continued to crackle. All they needed was for Richard to get out an acoustic guitar and start with the words, "Once upon a time."

'The 1066 group aren't just power-hungry, greedy people. They have an occult side to their nature.'

'Occult?'

'They believe in the power of the paranormal. Ritualistic practices handed down through the generations, from the Norman times. They believe the rituals will give them a stronger grip on Britain.'

Another beer came his way. Tony ripped off the ring pull and drank some, grimacing as he did. 'So you expect me to believe the 1066 group are dabbling in the occult? That's nonsense. Rituals? In the twenty-first century? Are these people cranks?'

Nobody laughed. A shiver went up Tony's spine.

'The ritual to reaffirm their power is performed by the club members at certain times of the year. It's done to appease the gods. Without the reaffirming ritual, they believe their privileged positions will disappear.'

Tony shook his head. 'I need some fresh air.' He stumbled towards the exit and yanked the door open. The star-lit sky shone on his face as he reflected about what he'd just heard. Together with the visions he'd been experiencing, his version of reality was rapidly turning upside down.

The cool air cleared Tony's head, and he went back into the cabin. It occurred to him that the Normans were Christians during their dominant historical period. The countless cathedrals built around the country were a testament to that. He took a seat beside Richard. 'What you're saying makes no sense.'

'What do you mean?'

'Normans weren't pagans. They were God-fearing Christians. You mentioned appeasing the gods.'

Richard looked impressed with Tony's insight and nodded. 'Yes, that's right. But in the Norman heyday, the higher members of their society practiced Nordic pagan rituals in secret. I'm sure you're aware the Normans are the direct descendants of the Vikings.'

Tony let out a crude laugh. 'I'm finding it hard to believe that these men engage in this sort of thing.'

'That's not all. Before the reaffirming ritual begins, a mass orgy takes place; high class prostitutes get bussed in and dressed up as Norman nobility. Once the sexual empowerment reaches its peak, the women are thrown out of the building.'

'So the sex makes the reaffirming ritual more powerful? Are you winding me up?'

'There's more. The Knights of Bayeux gather their enemies before the ritual. Sometimes, they take people off the streets.'

'Hold on a minute, where's this leading?'

'The victims get stripped naked, put into an old sack, gagged, bound, and put on the stage upstairs. One of the members dresses in Norman battle dress and wears a black executioner's mask. He cuts the victims' throats. They believe human sacrifice makes them invincible and that the gods will be on their side, no matter what. Sacrificing humans is the ultimate offering to appease them.'

Tony's face turned sickly white. He didn't want to end up as a sacrifice for some deranged Freemasons.

'So, why didn't the Knights of Bayeux sacrifice Veronica? Why didn't they take her as a captive?' He sat up straight. 'They said we're being watched, so why aren't we chained up in a makeshift prison somewhere, waiting to get our throats cut?'

'That was a warning,' Bob said. 'Perhaps they had bigger fish to contend with.'

Richard stood up close to where Bob sat. 'Their warning backfired, seeing as we've got some of their senior officials now.'

Tony half-smiled. 'I think we can assume we're their enemies now?'

John burped. 'Yeah, and we'd better make sure they don't capture us or our families. We don't want them ending up in a human sacrifice ritual, do we?'

The conversation drifted back to a drunken reverie, a welcome diversion from reality. Tony's worries floated away. All he wanted to do now was get drunk. He lobbed an empty can at Bob and missed. 'Who's up for getting pissed then?'

Hands rose in unison, and they all laughed. It was going to be a long night.

17

The alarm clock Bob had brought rang at ten in the morning. To Tony, it sounded like a fire alarm. He leaned over the side of the bed, retching and coughing, drawing him some unwanted attention from others, who were just as hungover as he was.

Tony strained and groaned as he got out of bed in just his underwear. He stumbled towards the backdoor, tripping over someone's boot along the way, heading to the toilet. The cold morning air assaulted him. His feet numbed as they crunched along the hardened frost on the dirt. He opened the door and threw up over the toilet seat. Dizziness overwhelmed him, and he threw up again. Sweat trickled down his forehead as he reached for the toilet roll and wiped the seat.

On his eager return to the hut, Tony noticed a few of his colleagues were still lying in their sleeping bags. There were strained faces and bear-like moans all around.

Bob was the only one who got up and dressed. He stood in the centre of the cabin with his hands on his hips. 'Come on, you lazy bastards, we've got a whole day of planning and analysing ahead of us – and I've got the perfect hangover cure.'

Curses, moans, and heavy yawns answered back. Tony glanced at Bob with glazed, blurry vision. 'I just want to sleep, Bob.'

Bob looked chirpy and full of life. He stretched his arms upward and ran on the spot. It was inconceivable considering how much he had drunk – they had all drunk – the previous night.

Stephen sat upright. He gagged a few times and picked his nose. 'Bob, what are you doing?'

Bob grinned. 'Well, my fellow weaklings – who clearly *can't* take their booze – there's a lake not far from here. We'll all going for a nice little swim. It's just what you idiots need. Don't forget to bring your towels.'

Bob walked over to each of the men and gave them a kick in the shin. 'Come on, for fuck's sake. What's wrong with you people? Get off your arses and *move*!'

Everyone got up and dressed for the trek to the lake. Stephen tripped over as he attempted to put on his trousers. John put on his top inside out. They looked a shambles as they followed Bob outside. It was the last thing any of them – with the exception of Bob – wanted to do.

They followed a flattened dirt path up steep slippery hills, passing through a mix of bare trees and evergreens with thick foliage on either side, but Tony was in no state to appreciate the scenery; he still felt intoxicated.

Stephen ran behind a tree and threw up. When he came back, he wiped his chin. His skin was a bloodless white.

Tony slapped him on the back. 'Blimey, mate, I thought I was bad. Bet you feel better now?'

Stephen offered a half-smile but said nothing.

Bob had a wicked grin on his face. He seemed to be enjoying playing the role of chief tormentor. 'Come on, lads, no slacking. You want to feel better, don't you?'

Jim's head lolled downward. He looked lifeless and grey. 'Yeah, but not like this. You ex-SAS types piss me off sometimes.'

Even though it was March, the trees showed no signs of sprouting leaves. As the group reached the peak of the path, the lake became visible. It looked about a quarter of a mile wide. The water was still and the wind minimal.

Bob didn't wait around. He stripped off his clothes and dove into the lake. His head surfaced a moment later, his eyes wide with zest. He gasped for air. Richard followed suit. Tony and the other men remained on the bank.

'Come on, you load of wankers. Are you going to dive in or what?' Bob said. 'Don't stand there like a load of losers. Get the fuck in!'

Tony stripped. Shivering, with hunched shoulders and with no sign of the enthusiasm Bob had shown, he jumped into the lake, taking a huge breath as he landed in the cold, unforgiving water. His face turned bright red, and his eyes widened. It felt like a thousand knives had pierced his skin. He wanted to cry out in pain as his body numbed, but he knew the teasing would be merciless.

There were shrieks and cries as the other men jumped in. Bob laughed at them all. 'I would gamble that your heads feel clearer now.'

No one responded; the icy water had taken their breaths away.

The torturous swim finally came to an end, and Tony stood shivering on the bank as he dried himself off. Bob's hangover remedy did what he said it would. His head was clearer; his hangover had more or less gone, and his thoughts returned to their war against the 1066 group. He wondered what Bob had planned for their next strike. They had to keep the momentum going now they had started. If they eased up, it would give the 1066 group a chance to retaliate.

Once everyone had dried off and gotten dressed, they headed back to the cabin. They all appeared more alive and alert after their swim.

As Tony entered the cabin, he noticed a large wooden crate he hadn't seen before. Bob clapped his hands and asked for everyone's attention. 'We have another mission to plan for. We've got to strike hard at the enemy.'

The cabin hushed. Bob was skilled at getting the full attention from his audience, with or without a drill. 'My sources have informed me that Murphy's drug distribution is nationwide now. Addiction is increasing across the country, and the crime rate is worsening.

'Giles Campbell confirmed what we suspected, and their plan is fast becoming a reality. Not only that, but competing gangs are being wiped out. Those who surrender to Murphy's demands are getting added to the payroll, allowing him to create an all-powerful criminal army – right across the country.'

Stephen frowned. 'It's amazing how quickly Murphy's doing this.'

Richard scowled. 'When you've got the full force of the law behind you, there's nothing to stop you, is there?'

The cabin fell silent. Tony pondered on what they'd discussed so far. Like Stephen, he was surprised at the speed Murphy was working at. A jolt shot through his head, and his vision doubled. The room lurched, and he grabbed the shelf beside him.

Bob glanced at Tony. 'Has that dip done something to you? You look as if you're in your own little world.'

'Just tired.'

'Right, well, let's continue discussing our next manoeuvre, shall we? The bulk of Murphy's drugs are stored in a large industrial warehouse in Poplar, close to the River Thames, and we're going to torch the place to let them know we're here to cause as much damage as possible. We'll keep to the same teams as before, so Tony and Jim will be with me. The rest of you are going to raid another of Murphy's brothels. This one's in Knightsbridge. Shut it down and take the cash from the safe, but be careful – security will be tighter by now.'

Bob rummaged through one of his bags and pulled out a blue vinyl clip folder. He handed it to Richard. 'All the information you need is in here. Any questions, just ask.'

Richard skimmed through the folder. 'Seems fine, Bob. We'll go through it later.'

Bob pointed to the box. 'We have, from the proceeds of our labour, some better hardware now – military grade. It should make our forthcoming missions a lot easier. A friend of mine brought this in while we were trekking through the forest.'

Tony smiled. 'Come on, Bob. Don't keep us waiting.'

Bob pried the lid of the crate open with a crowbar but didn't lift the lid. He shook his head. 'No, not just yet. I have a surprise for you all first.' He pulled out his phone and made a call. 'Okay, you can bring them in now.'

For a moment, Tony thought something sinister was about to happen, then the door of the cabin opened and Veronica, Charlie, and Doris walked in with the families of the seven men.

Veronica's eyes lit up, and she ran to Tony. Tony couldn't believe they were all here. He embraced Veronica in a passionate clinch, feeling a fresh spark of life flowing through him. 'It's so good to see you again, Tony.'

They kissed each other, unconcerned about their display of affection in front of the others. Tony was lost for words and overwhelmed by happiness. It felt wonderful to be around the people who mattered.

Charlie tapped Tony on the shoulder. 'Has everything been good, son?'

Tony pulled away from Veronica and turned to face him. 'Yeah, Uncle Charlie, everything's great. I can't elaborate further, but yeah, its fine.'

Charlie hugged him – and Doris too. They exchanged a little small talk, then Tony glanced at Bob. 'Bob, is it okay for me and Veronica to go for a walk?'

'Yeah, no problem. But don't stray too far.'

Tony grabbed Veronica's hand and led her into the Forest. After a five-minute walk, they slipped behind a tree, kissing and groping each other. Tony felt a desperate need to be close to her. He spotted a dense-looking scrub and led her towards it.

Tony and Veronica arrived back in the cabin looking like a couple of love-struck teenagers giggling, laughing, and acting silly.

Charlie pulled Tony away from the crowd and asked him if he'd like to go outside. Tony nodded and followed him out of the cabin.

'Bob seems like a good bloke,' Charlie said. 'We were just chatting.'

'Yeah he is. He's ex-SAS.'

'Blimey, you can't get any better than that, can you?'

Tony frowned. 'Is there a problem, Uncle Charlie? I mean, you've pulled me outside for a reason. I hope it's nothing too serious?'

'No, nothing like that. Bob knew everything about me – my past and present. It made me uncomfortable.'

'He checks up on everything; he's thorough like that. It's nothing personal.'

Charlie nodded. 'I'm not aware of the full extent of what's going on, but a few people from the bad, old days got murdered the other week. There's a lot of villains out there shitting themselves.'

'Yeah. I can't comment, but I hope things will get back to normal soon.'

'Just be careful out there. All right?'

'I will.'

The family get-togethers ended, and there were tearful departures as everyone said their goodbyes. Tony embraced Veronica, never wanting to let her go. 'This'll be over soon,' he told her, hoping it wasn't an empty

SERFDOM AND DISORDER

promise.

Tears welled up in her eyes as she nodded. Tony let her go, and she kissed him one last time.

The cabin felt like an empty shell now that their families had gone. A soulless desert. Tony felt drained. Seeing Veronica, Charlie, and Doris had meant the world to him. He yearned to get back to the booze to blot out some of the emptiness he felt and stared at the cans of lager, not really knowing what to do next.

Bob stood up, looking as tall and proud as ever. 'Come on, lads. I know this is hard, but we've got to give our attention to what lays before us. Its gut-wrenching, I know, but we have to fulfill our objectives.'

Stephen walked over to Bob. 'So, where's all this high-tech weaponry then? I know you're gagging to show us your latest toys.'

Bob took off the lid of the wooden crate he had pried open earlier and took out seven AR-15 rifles. There was a large number of hand and stun grenades, too, together with mortars, smoke bombs, night vision goggles, and two Carl Gustav portable anti-tank rocket launchers. They had quite an armoury at their disposal now.

Tony stared at it. The arms were a definite morale boost, an opinion the other men seemed to share.

Jim laughed. 'Fucking hell, Bob, are we buying a tank next?'

John took a swig of water from a bottle. 'I never thought we'd get this much. How did you manage it?'

'Being in the SAS for some years helped. Not only do we have new weapons, I got us a couple of new vans too. I've a friend who works for a Vauxhall dealership, and he gave me a special deal. I would gamble you're all eager to play boy soldiers now, aren't you?'

Everyone nodded. Bob had been right in his assumption, and his face beamed.

Simon Gatting grinned. 'So, when's the next mission?'

The men laughed as they handled the weapons and pretended to shoot at a target. Tony couldn't wait to get started. He put the Carl Gustav rocket launcher on his shoulder and put on a tough soldier face, then questioned himself. This wasn't a game – they could get killed, or maimed.

SERFDOM AND DISORDER

18

Morning within the New Forest was a misty affair. There was no sun, just dim skies and the outlines of trees. The two teams, dressed in navy-blue overalls, assembled together in their new Vauxhall black Vivaro vans. There was a lot of backslapping and handshaking as everyone wished each other well on their allotted tasks.

The two-van convoy headed out of the forest's dark and winding roads into reality, ready to face the concrete jungle that awaited them. Tony had a slight sinking feeling at leaving the forest and rural life behind. He preferred the natural world to urbanised life. 'God, I hate London. I detest the place.'

Bob smiled. 'Well, there'll be plenty of time to get used to these surroundings. We won't be leaving the cabin for a while yet. Unless we get shot and killed, or arrested – or worse still, getting sacrificed.'

Jim laughed. 'Don't like the prospect of getting my throat cut much. When I have a beer, it'll pour out of my throat.'

It felt strange listening to Jim and Bob's jovial and

light-hearted exchange in the lead-up to a situation that could get them all killed. The mission was no laughing matter. There were millions of pounds worth of drugs in the Poplar warehouse. Security was tight on all fronts, and it wouldn't be easy to raid. They had an arsenal of weapons with them, but they couldn't get complacent, especially after the raids at the brothels. Security would have been increased anywhere that Murphy had a stake.

Bob laughed. 'You look deep in thought, Tony. Anything you want to share with us? Or are you replaying the sex you had with Veronica yesterday?'

'We went for a walk in the forest. Nothing happened.'

Bob laughed even more. 'It was written all over your faces.'

Tony gave Bob a cool look. He wasn't the type to brag about his sexual conquests. He left that to the people he associated with in Plaistow. He loved Veronica and intended to marry her. There was no way he was going to talk about her in a degrading fashion – not to impress a load of testosterone-fuelled blokes.

The journey into London dragged; the only excitement came from the radio. Bob tuned the radio into a station that played hits from the sixties, seventies, and eighties. Everyone fell into their own little world as they drew closer to their target, as if the journey forced them to focus on what was in front of them.

As the van approached the entrance to Blackwall Tunnel on the south side of the River Thames, Tony felt jittery. Once they had driven through to the other side into Popular, his nerves multiplied; his right thigh muscle twitched, which he tried to subdue by whacking it with his fist. Images of Veronica flashed through his mind, and his old uncertainty returned. He wanted to go back to the cabin in the New Forest, but it couldn't happen, not yet anyway.

'Almost there,' Bob said. 'Get your weapons ready. Remember your roles and, more importantly, don't shit yourself in the thick of the action.'

The van pulled into the middle of the run-down Lansbury Estate, an area with a reputation for being a no-go zone. Flats, houses, and maisonettes were heaped on top of each other.

They parked around the corner from Murphy's warehouse and got out of the van, lifting their large canvas sports bag from the back. Bob whistled a tune as he walked, trying his best to appear casual and laid back.

Tony glanced around. There was a gang of youths hanging around in the distance. They eyeballed him and his colleagues with narrowed eyes, curled lips, and frowns. There were ten of them in all, each of them dressed in baggy trousers, hoodies, and baseball caps. 'Bob, that mob to your right are giving us the stare eye treatment.'

'Just ignore them. If we don't bother them, they won't bother us.'

Tony wasn't so sure. Rawstone Walk wasn't so different from this estate, and he understood how these people worked. These fuckers were territorial and would view their arrival as encroaching on their turf.

Bob veered away from the gang, heading in a different direction. Tony and Jim followed. They walked past rows of the concrete hellholes and the shoddy-looking people hanging around the street corners.

Rubbish littered the road side. The smell of cannabis was rife. A man in a blue tracksuit staggered around the corner and approached them. 'Oi, mate, got a light and a fag?'

Bob stared at the man. His eyes narrowed and his mouth tightened. 'I don't smoke.'

'Don't smoke… you cunt. I don't—'

Bob grabbed the man's throat and squeezed. The man choked and gagged, his eyes bulging as his face turned blue.

The group of youths took a few steps towards them as Bob karate-chopped the back of the drunk's neck. He fell to the floor with a thud.

Bob glanced at Tony and Jim. 'Let's go.'

Their pace quickened. Their target was a patch of wasteland beyond the estate.

Jim frowned. 'Coming here during the day was a bad move. Wrong place, wrong time. Too many eyes'

'Yeah, I think you're right,' Bob said. 'Let's get out of here.'

They turned back and headed back to the van. The gang of youths approached them, faces marred with anger. Some of them had pulled knives out of their pockets; others carried baseball bats.

Tony turned to Bob. 'What are we going to do? We can't shoot them in broad daylight.'

'I'll sort it.' He smiled. 'This is nothing.'

Tony didn't share his confidence and placed his hand in his bag, gripping hold of the gun in case things turned nasty.

Bob smiled. 'Don't get your knickers in a twist.' He put his hand in a pocket of his overalls and pulled out two devices. 'Don't worry. One's a stun grenade, and the other's a smoke bomb.'

Stun grenades had the power to disorientate, causing temporary deafness and blindness, and he tossed it at the approaching mob. Before they could scatter, it went off, knocking the kids to the floor. They rolled in agony, clutching their hands to their ears. But Bob hadn't finished yet. He lobbed the smoke bomb at them, engulfing the area, then urged Tony and Jim to hurry to the van.

People came out of their homes; others looked out of their windows. There was shouting and screaming everywhere.

They jumped in the van, and Bob reversed out of the parking space, spun it around, and sped out of the estate with a high-pitched screech.

'That was hardcore,' Tony said as he gripped hold of the edge of his seat.

'That was nothing. A stroll in the park.'

Jim leaned forwards. 'I'm glad I don't go for walks in your park.'

Bob laughed. 'I'd better find somewhere quiet and change the number plates. Quite a few people saw us.'

Tony gritted his teeth, but he was grateful to be with someone who knew what they were doing. 'You know your stuff, don't you?'

'When you've been in the situations I've been in, it comes natural.'

Bob pulled the van into an empty street. He jumped out of the driver's door, ran to the van's rear, and opened the back door. Within no time at all, he had the number plates changed and discarded the old ones in a plastic wheelie bin. He nodded to Tony and Jim. 'We'd better get out of these overalls. We don't want the police pulling us.'

They placed the overalls in their canvas bags. The van moved off. This time, Bob headed to a location Tony and Jim didn't know about, looking irate as he navigated the inner London streets. He clutched the steering wheel a little bit tighter than before. 'I can't believe how fucking stupid I am. Planning to raid the warehouse in the day. What an idiot!'

'Where are we going now the mission's off?' Tony asked.

'Kent. Good friend of mine lives there.'

An hour later, they arrived at the beautiful village of Pembury. The countryside looked lush, green, and beautiful. It was like being in another world, a welcome relief to claustrophobic London. Everything looked so peaceful and easygoing.

Tony rolled down the window and took in the scenery. 'Wow, this beats where I live.'

He would have loved to live in a place like Pembury. The cold and unwelcoming streets of East London had never appealed to him, but not having much in the way of money limited his options. He was stuck with the horrid council estate in Plaistow.

Bob pulled into a red-bricked driveway on the grounds of a four-bedroom detached house. It looked as if it was built in the nineteen fifties. The house had a warm feel about it. From the outside, everything looked spotless, clean, and tidy.

'Who's this friend of yours, then, Bob?' Tony asked.

'A good friend from my days of serving Britain.'

SERFDOM AND DISORDER

Bob led the way up the paved walkway to the front door. A beefy lumberjack of a man answered. 'Davis, good to see you again.'

'It's good to see you too, Ogden.'

Like Bob, Mickey Ogden was an SAS veteran, serving in missions the British government had assigned them. They greeted each other with bear hugs and laughter. Mickey escorted everyone to the living room, explaining that his wife and two children were out shopping.

Bob grinned. 'I was just passing and thought I'd call in. When was the last time we saw each other?'

'Must be about two years now.'

Mickey escorted them to the lounge area, gesturing for them to take a seat on his beige-coloured fabric sofa and chairs, and then offered each of them a glass of Scotch. They raised a glass and toasted to 'continued health and success.' The others echoed Mickey and shouted cheers afterwards.

Mickey and Bob downed their whiskey in one go. Tony glanced at Jim, shrugged his shoulders, and poured the drink down his throat. The warmth hit his chest and spread to his face. He tried to say something, but it was too much effort. A sudden rush hit his head.

Bob and Mickey laughed. 'You can't handle the hard stuff, can you?' Bob said. 'Good thing you weren't in my regiment. The men would have given you a lot of stick.'

The laughter and mimicry continued, together with the odd war story thrown in from Bob and Mickey. It was a pleasant diversion from the botched raid on Murphy's warehouse.

'So, what's the real purpose of this visit?' asked Mickey. 'What trouble have you got yourself into?'

'You always were good at sniffing out bullshit.' Bob grinned. 'Some plans backfired this morning.'

'Not another one of those mercenary missions, is it?'

Bob outlined the details from Murphy to the link with the 1066 group, the Home Office, and the Metropolitan Police. Mickey poured himself another whiskey and downed it as Bob outlined their plan to take the warehouse.

'That 1066 group is unbelievable,' Mickey said. 'There's no way we can allow that to happen. I don't want my kids growing up in work camps.'

'There's a mission tonight. Would you be willing to join us?'

'I can't walk away from this, so, yeah, you can count me in.'

SERFDOM AND DISORDER

19

The mission on Murphy's warehouse resumed at midnight, only this time, Mickey Ogden was part of the team. It was cold and frosty, and Lansbury Estate was empty. Tony, Jim, Micky, and Bob dressed in a fresh set of navy-blue overalls. They carried their canvas sports bags, ready to receive whatever providence would throw at them.

Bob only had weapons for the original team, so Mickey had brought his own arsenal along. Bob's eyes widened. 'Blimey, Mick, you've got better weapons than us. Are you sure you're not doing any mercenary work yourself?'

Mickey smiled, winked, and said nothing further.

Tony wiped a trickle of sweat from his forehead as they drew closer to the warehouse. He glanced at his watch a few times and surveyed the twenty-foot perimeter fence. It looked like an imposing proposition to get over. There were CCTV cameras all around, but Bob could easily fix them.

Bob pulled some respiratory masks out of his bag and handed one each to Jim, Tony, and Mickey. 'We might need these. If any bullets hit the packets of drugs they'll be a dust cloud of heroin and cocaine floating around. Anyone breathes anything like that in, they'll be bang in trouble.' Bob gave a fiendish smile. 'The party's about to begin, fellas.'

Tony rubbed his neck as he stopped outside the main gate of the warehouse. He felt secure having two ex-SAS men in their team. If things got tough, at least he was with people who could look after themselves.

Bob slapped Tony's shoulder. 'Don't look so down. It's a stroll around the block for me and Mickey.'

Bob produced a thick set of heavy bulk croppers from his bag. The main padlock, attached to a chunky metal chain, broke off with ease. Bob eased the gate open and slipped inside, the others following not too far behind. The next thing out of Bob's bag was the Carl Gustav anti-tank rocket launcher. He placed the rocket launcher on his shoulder, aimed the device, and fired at the warehouse entrance. A rocket ejected at breakneck speed. The resulting bang echoed across a wide radius. If anything woke up the estate, that would be it.

Mickey took a L9A1 51-millimetre light mortar from his bag, and as the fire raged, he aimed the mortar at the security hut with deadly accuracy. The single-storey building disintegrated on impact; debris and fire exploded into the air.

Bob darted forward. 'Well, that's the CCTV problem resolved. Let's get moving.'

Two of Murphy's thugs, dressed in casual attire, ran outside the warehouse. They looked stunned and stumbled around for a brief second, but upon seeing the team approach, they raised their pump-action shotguns and fired.

Bob, Tony and Jim fired shots with their AR-15 semi-automatic rifles, while Mickey returned fire with his Enfield SA80 assault rifle. Noise, smoke, and bullets rebounded in all directions. The No Mercy men were picked off before they had a chance to retaliate. Blood splattered the black tarmac floor as the two men fell to the ground.

Tony experienced an adrenaline rush as they continued forwards. He had total respect for Bob and the way he did things. *He's a fucking psycho; there's no stopping him.*

They put on their respiratory masks before entering the warehouse. Tony's senses alerted him to the potential for an ambush. He kept his finger on the trigger of his AR-15 and didn't dare loosen his grip; this was his life saver.

The warehouse was enormous and had dozens of racks packed with drugs. Tony could only imagine how much money the shelves contained.

Shots came from every direction. One zipped past Tony's ear, and bullets impacted the walls. Everyone dove for cover as the bullets hit the boxes and bags full of drugs. Narcotic dust clouds drifted across the warehouse. One of the No Mercy men called out to them. 'Whoever you bastards are, this is the last moment you've got alive in this world. There's no escape from here. You're all dead.'

Bob split the four of them into two groups. Tony went with Bob, while Jim and Mickey moved in the opposite direction. Tony crouched low, following Bob into a dusty cloud of uncertainty. His legs felt shaky, and his heart raced as shots went off all around him.

'We'll flush these scum bags out, don't worry about that.'

Tony followed Bob like a cub follows its mother: 'I hope you're right – for both of our sakes.'

'These idiots are nothing.'

Tony could just make out a No Mercy thug. He fired rapid bursts at the outline. The target fell. Bob patted him on the back.

Bullets continued to zip past Tony as two more No Mercy men appeared through the haze. Bob flinched and dropped his weapon. He held a hand over his shoulder to stem the blood pouring from it. Tony squeezed the trigger; the two gangsters fell.

Bob Patted Tony on the shoulder and pointed to a set of shelves. 'Get that can of petrol.'

Tony did as Bob asked and darted back to him. Bob leaned against a wall and pulled out an anti-tank rocket warhead from his bag. 'Pour the petrol from the exit area up to the shelf in front of me. Leave the canister on the shelf next to the oxy-acetylene bottles and take this warhead.'

Tony followed Bob's instructions to the letter. When he'd finished his job, Tony tried to drag Bob up from the floor, which wasn't an easy task. He exerted every inch of strength into the effort. Dizziness hit him, and his strength diminished, but he eventually pulled a semi-conscious Bob upright and dragged him towards the exit.

Bob's eyes were half open. 'Come on, you big softie, let's get this sorted.'

Tony half-smiled. That was what he liked about Bob;

he was cool in tense situations, allaying Tony's dread and fear.

Bob propped himself against the debris-laden exit and shouted for Jim and Mickey to get out of the warehouse. Bob handed Tony a cigarette lighter. He found some cloth and clicked the lighter, then tossed the fiery cloth at the line of petrol. Fire soared down the line Tony had sprayed on the floor, its orange glow spread at speed.

Bob raged. 'We'd better get the fuck out of here!'

Tony spotted a wheelbarrow near the exit. He grabbed hold of Bob and placed him on top of it. He pushed it as fast as he could, grimacing under the strain to his arms, but it was such a relief to be outside breathing clean air.

When he was some distance away, he set the wheelbarrow down and glanced back at the warehouse. Jim and Mickey were running towards them. Sweat poured out of every region of Tony's body as he struggled to lift the wheelbarrow again and get himself and Bob to safety. He couldn't see any of Murphy's thugs.

The explosion moments later was thunderous. Shock waves spread outward, shattering windows on the surrounding estate. Orange flames and black plumes of smoke engulfed the warehouse. Car and shop alarms rang from all around.

Bob's face illuminated with excitement. 'What a fucking buzz that was!'

Mickey tapped Tony on the shoulder. 'Want a hand?'

He took the wheelbarrow from Tony, and they ran as a secondary explosion rang out. People congregated on the nearby streets, shouting obscenities at them. Some people threw bottles.

After what seemed like hours, they arrived at the van. Mickey shouted. 'Jim, put your toe down and get us out of here.'

Jim did as he was asked, and the van sped away under a barrage of bottles and bricks. Bob announced that they would have to pull over and change their number plates again.

Tony couldn't contain his words anymore. 'My heart was in my mouth back there. I thought we'd all get killed. Look at my hands; they're still shaking.'

Bob and Mickey laughed. To them, it probably wasn't anything extraordinary.

Mickey patted Tony on the back. 'These blokes from Civvy Street make me laugh. But fair play to you, you did a good job tonight.'

'I'll second that. Jim and Tony did us proud. You held your nerve.'

A surge of self-confidence filled Tony.

They headed to Kent first to take Mickey back home and then returned to the base camp in the New Forest – their home for the foreseeable future.

Tony was relieved to be back in the New Forest and relative safety, but he felt drained. His body and mind cried out for sleep, and he yawned loudly.

The other team had returned earlier and were settled around the fire. Tony glanced around the cabin. 'Where's Stephen?'

Everyone appeared a little uncomfortable at the mention of Stephen's name. Richard had a solemn look on his face. 'Nothing happened to Stephen, but his dad died. He's gone to the safe house.'

'On his own?' Bob asked.

Richard bristled. 'I offered to go with him, but he was adamant he wanted to go alone.'

'Don't you know how dangerous—' Bob sighed. 'It's not your fault.'

'Nothing could have stopped him leaving!'

'Okay, keep your calm. Let's just hope no one catches up with him.'

Bob eased himself into a seat. 'So, how did Murphy's whorehouse go?'

John drew a heavy breath. 'The mission was a success. The place had extra security, but it didn't stop us. We emptied the safe and burnt the place down.'

'No prisoners?'

'Nothing this time. The place was full of wealthy foreigners. Not much value for our fight.'

'So, the 1066 group have realised how dangerous it is to be at one of Murphy's whorehouses.'

'We've achieved a lot. At least we've come out of these clashes with no one getting killed.'

'I agree. Apart from me getting shot in the shoulder, we're doing fine.'

Bob glanced at Richard. 'I assume you've done basic first aid as part of your Royal Marine training?'

Richard nodded.

'Good, there's a first aid kit in the cupboard.'

Richard patched Bob up as best he could, all while Bob sat on his seat as if nothing had happened.

'Thanks for that, Rich. Can you call a doctor I know? His number's on my phone – under doctor, funnily enough.' He pulled his mobile out of his pocket and handed it over. 'He's just the man for these situations. You can get a signal from here; there's a mast not too far away.'

'Where do you want me to meet him, if he agrees to come?'

'There's a layby just before the road meets the A31. Tell him to meet you there.'

'Has he got far to come?'

'He's about a forty-minute drive away. He lives in Surrey.'

'I'll park up at the layby and give him directions.'

Richard made the call. The doctor agreed to meet up at the designated spot.

Everyone in the cabin drank beer, apart from Bob. Most of the men looked on edge, and Tony was worried about Stephen. Only Bob seemed relaxed.

After a few more cans of beer had been consumed, Tony got up from his seat to go to the toilet outside for a piss. He also needed some fresh air.

Although it was spring, the nights were still cold. He shivered in the portable toilet as he attempted to get his piss over with quickly. Relieved to have completed the task, he zipped up his flies on his jeans. The pale-faced man in the black jumpsuit appeared from out of nowhere.

Tony jerked back. *You bastard. You made me jump. Your timing's impeccable, as always.*

'Sorry, just to let you know we've had trouble with communications again. It's working at the moment, but we are oblivious when it might go again.'

What the hell are you going on about?

'We're making sure you're handling everything okay.'

Who the fuck are you?

The man's face drooped, and he looked uncomfortable. He evaporated into thin air, and Tony shook his head, doubting his sanity again. He bashed his head against the toilet to check he was awake and not dreaming.

Tony returned to the warmth of the cabin and attempted to forget everything over a few beers. He took off his boots and stretched out his legs before the fire, intending to defrost his toes.

Richard arrived back at the cabin with the doctor, who injected Bob with an anaesthetic before taking the bullet out. Before the doctor left, he handed some painkillers to Richard.

Tony's stretched his arms and yawned. He dosed off and then snapped out of it. 'Sorry, people, my eyes won't stay open any longer. I'm going to my sleeping bag to get some sleep.'

A glassy-eyed Jim responded. 'Yeah, good idea, I think I'll do the same shortly.'

The drinking ended. Everyone wandered over to their sleeping bags, all looking for a decent night's sleep.

20

Tony's body stiffened when he opened his eyes to face another day. His head was still clouded from a vivid dream, in which both he and Veronica had run away from a gigantic snowball that threatened to crush them.

He sat upright, his eyes strained after his deep sleep. He still felt exhausted and felt an urge to go to the lake for a swim. He struggled to get out of his sleeping bag, wincing as he did.

Once he was fully dressed, Tony glanced around the cabin to see if anyone else was awake. They weren't, not even Bob. He squinted at his watch. It was around seven thirty.

Tony crept towards the cabin door. He didn't want a load of men blaming him for interrupting their sleep. As he drew nearer to the door, the floor creaked. He froze, not wanting to look around to see if he had woken anyone, then headed out of the hut.

It was a crisp morning – bright sunshine but with traces of frost, as if winter refused to let go of its icy grip. Tony strolled through the forest. There were birds of different descriptions – fire crests, hawfinches, lesser-spotted woodpeckers, to name but a few – going about their business. The occasional grey squirrel darted past, desperate to get out of the way of human contact. Tony loved the countryside, the sound of birds, the trees, and the crunch of twigs under foot, together with the wooded smell. It felt so tranquil and life-affirming.

Tony reached the lake. The morning was cold, and the lake looked uninviting. He stripped off anyway and stood naked, shivering, full of apprehension. He closed his eyes, counted to ten, and dove in.

On impact with the water, the cold swamped his body. A surge of blood rushed to his head as he gasped.

After swimming in the most enduring of conditions for around five minutes, Tony's mind cleared and his body surged with life. Bob's hangover cure worked a treat.

He dried himself off and dressed, feeling warmer now he was out of the lake, and enjoyed a leisurely stroll back to the cabin. This time, he took in the pleasant surroundings. He had enjoyed his swim; a perfect way to start his day.

'Psst, Tony. Over here.'

He snapped out of his daydream and turned towards the voice. Bob had positioned himself behind a shrub and was waving his arm to attract Tony's attention.

A sense of unease enveloped Tony. He sprinted to where Bob crouched. A shot rang out. The bullet impacted near Tony's foot, and he ran with every inch of energy he had, diving into a ditch. He landed badly, cutting his cheek and forehead as he brushed the side of the scrub, then crawled forwards on all fours. He was covered in mud, twigs, and aches and pains, heading towards Bob, although he wasn't sure it was Bob pissing him about.

Bob held a pistol in his hand. Tony stared at him, searching his face for answers.

'The cabin got raided,' Bob whispered. 'I saw you leaving and was about to follow when I heard a racket and ran for cover. There was about fifteen of them – all armed. There was no time to warn the others. They got them, Tony. They cuffed them and marched them off. They set the vans ablaze too.'

He held his pistol up. 'I only had this one on me. It would have been foolish to shoot. I wouldn't have had much chance against all those raiders.' He glanced towards the cabin. 'I think they're searching for us. They know how many of us there are.' He ran a hand over his head. 'I can't believe this is happening.'

'You'd better fucking believe it, pal.'

A man with dark, emotionless eyes stepped in front of them, aiming an automatic rifle at Tony's head.

Tony froze. Sweat trickled down his face as he stared at Bob, feeling the cold edge of the steel barrel against his temple.

'Drop the pistol, or I'll blow his brains out!'

Bob eyeballed the man, appearing as calm as ever. Tony sensed something was about to happen and closed his eyes. He heard the pistol fall to the ground a short distance away. He opened his eyes again and watched as Bob raised his arms in surrender.

The gunman's face screwed up like a ball of tinfoil. He gestured for Tony to stand next to Bob.

'Okay, you pair of cunts, walk back to the cabin. I want no silly business. I'll be right behind you. Any nonsense, and I'll shoot.'

Tony and Bob had no choice but to follow his instructions and walk towards the cabin. The forest had a strange and eerie feel to it. It was quiet; nature's inhabitants had fallen silent.

Bob spoke casually. 'I take it you're from the No Mercy firm, then?'

'That's right, and you'll have more of an idea about us in the coming hours, that's for sure.'

'So how did you discover where to find us?'

'Stephen Downer. We captured and tortured him. The bastard couldn't stop talking once he started. It was fun to watch. I enjoyed it.'

Tony stumbled. The thought of Stephen being tortured twisted his stomach. He retched, and his face lost colour. Veronica and everyone else could be in danger. He glanced at Bob, who winked back at him.

As the journey back to the hut continued, Bob began talking to the gunman. 'So, looks like you've beaten our firm then?'

The gunman smirked. 'Yeah, seems that way. Your little game didn't last too long did it.'

'What happens to us now?'

'I don't know mate. Whatever it is, it won't be too pleasant.'

From nowhere Bob did a reverse kick straight into the groin of the gunman. The man grimaced and shrieked in pain. The automatic rifle he carried dropped to the ground.

Tony reacted first; he picked up the firearm and put two shots into their former captive's torso. Murphy's henchman laid on the dirt path, eyes motionless, blood seeping out of his mouth and body.

Bob snatched the gun out of Tony's hand. 'Follow me.'

The forest sounds returned as Tony and Bob ran across the crunchy terrain for a further ten minutes. They stopped and hid behind a thick scrub of vegetation. 'They must have heard those shots,' Bob said. 'I hope they head this way so we can shoot them. Oh, I liked your reaction to that scumbag getting kicked in the bollocks; it was spot on. I'll make an elite soldier out of you yet.'

Bob grinned and raised his finger to his mouth. They waited for their moment to strike. Tony's thoughts returned to Stephen and his family, who might well be at risk of capture too. He clenched his fist and pushed it against his forehead.

They waited patiently for a further fifteen minutes, expecting Murphy's hitmen to appear, but no one came. Time dragged on, and the dread in Tony's mind eased. He breathed a heavy sigh of relief. There would be no more bloodshed. Well, not for the moment.

Bob whispered. 'I think we can breathe a little easier. It doesn't look as if they want to risk any more casualties'

'What happens now? We've been through a pit of shit already. Where do we go from here?'

'Stop panicking for a start. When you've lived through what I've encountered, you know to have a plan B. I've had this situation planned out since the day we moved into the cabin.'

'What are you talking about?'

'A backup plan.'

'So, plan B?'

'We head back to London and meet a friend of mine from my old SAS days. I informed him I might visit, in case of an emergency.'

'Another ex-SAS veteran? What about Mickey? Will you tell him what's happened?'

'Course I will. But we have to get back to London first and meet my pal from yesteryear.'

Tony nodded and drew a deep breath. 'Our weapons were in the cabin—'

Bob grinned. 'Quit worrying. Now, come on, I've got a pal to hook up with, and it's a long walk to London.'

21

Tony and Bob had no money or possessions. The only way they could get back to London was through hitchhiking. It was both exhausting and arduous, but after three lifts from generous drivers, they made it to Paddington, in the west of the city.

Bob lead the way to his friend's house. 'His name's Harry Banks. He's in his early forties and is the most reliable person you could meet. If ever you're up to your neck in crap, Harry would back you all the way.'

He rang the doorbell, and a muscular man with short-cropped, grey hair answered the door. Harry beamed. 'Davis. Great to see you again. Come in.'

Harry patted Bob on the back. 'I assume plan B is in effect. What happens now?'

They sat in Harry's large, tiled kitchen. Bob scratched under his armpit as he described the affairs of the 1066 group and Murphy, together with everything else that had happened. Then, he outlined their next move. 'First, I'll phone the place where our prisoners are. We can't afford to lose them; they're invaluable to our cause. After that, we need to check out the safe house in Witham. If No Mercy or the 1066 group have found them, our families will be in danger. I hope for their sakes they haven't.'

'What about Mickey? Are we going to call him? We'll need him for what's in front of us, won't we?' said Tony.

'I'll do that now. He can be down here within the hour, and then we can get the ball rolling.'

Although he felt at ease with military professionals, Tony wasn't anywhere near their standard. They had all done their fair share of military action; whereas, his experience was limited to the couple of missions he had been involved in over the last two days.

Harry offered them a cup of coffee each. Even though Tony had never met Harry before, he found him easy to talk to and get along with. Tony didn't usually engage in shit talk, but on this occasion, he made an exception.

Bob yawned. 'I'll let you two carry on with your intellectual chit-chat. I think I'll have a sleep.'

Tony and Harry continued to talk while Bob snored away in the next room, sound asleep.

The doorbell rang. Harry went to the door, and Tony heard him say, 'Ogden, how ya doing, mate?'

Bob woke a short time later and came through to the living room to join them. He pulled out his phone. 'I've still got to make a call to the men holding our prisoners.' He strolled up to the window. 'Hello, Martin, it's Bob. Look, this is just a warning, but you might get raided by Murphy's henchmen or the Knights of Bayeux.'

Tony glanced at his brothers in arms. He couldn't believe how ordinary and normal they looked. Their appearances and mannerisms made them seem like every day, ordinary blokes, not ex-SAS.

Bob ended his call and rubbed his hands together. 'I think it's time we set off to Witham.'

They left Harry's house and got into Mickey's black Ford B-Max. Mickey turned on the radio, and they listened to some seventies rock. Tony tapped his fingers to the beat of the music on the interior car door. 'Wouldn't it be safer to phone the safe house first?' he asked Bob.

'We agreed there would be no telephone calls.'

Mickey navigated through the maze of London's streets, onto the orbital road, the M25, and onto the A12.

After a journey that lasted about an hour, through an empty motorway, they reached Fairplay House. Its usual function was to house kids taking trips from the East London borough of Newham, giving the youngsters an opportunity to go on field trips, canoeing, and a host of other outdoor events.

Harry parked a short distance away, down a country lane. Tony got out of the car and stretched his arms and legs, letting off a low-toned yawn. There were no streetlights, only the light of the moon. The outline of the house was just about visible. There wasn't a single light on, which was understandable considering the time.

The four men held their pistols at the ready as they approached the house, just in case there were any uninvited guests waiting for them. The only sound came from an owl and a gentle breeze.

Bob was the first to reach the main entrance. The others looked around for potential threats. The entrance door was ajar. Bob nudged it open. He glanced back at his colleagues with a look of anguish.

SERFDOM AND DISORDER

One by one, they followed Bob inside. 'Don't turn the lights on,' he said.

Tony whispered back. 'Why?'

'Because we don't want to give away our position.'

The rooms downstairs were empty, and Tony feared the worse. He was afraid that Veronica, Charlie, and Doris had been kidnapped. His heart pumped a little bit faster.

They crept up the stairs and continued their search. Each of the rooms they had checked so far had been empty. Tony cursed under his breath as they approached the final room. It didn't look hopeful.

Bob opened the final door and stepped inside. 'Turn the light on, Mick.'

The brightness was startling. In the far right-hand corner of the room, away from the curtained windows, a naked Stephen Downer hung lifeless on the end of a rope. His body was covered in cuts and bruises. A sign pinned on his chest read, '𝕴𝖊 𝖍𝖆𝖛𝖊 𝖙𝖆𝖐𝖊𝖓 𝖙𝖍𝖊 𝖕𝖊𝖔𝖕𝖑𝖊 𝖞𝖔𝖚 𝖑𝖔𝖛𝖊. 𝕿𝖍𝖊 𝖔𝖓𝖑𝖞 𝖜𝖆𝖞 𝖋𝖔𝖗 𝖆 𝖘𝖆𝖙𝖎𝖘𝖋𝖆𝖈𝖙𝖔𝖗𝖞 𝖈𝖔𝖓𝖈𝖑𝖚𝖘𝖎𝖔𝖓 𝖎𝖘 𝖆 𝖕𝖗𝖎𝖘𝖔𝖓𝖊𝖗 𝖊𝖝𝖈𝖍𝖆𝖓𝖌𝖊, 𝖔𝖗 𝖙𝖍𝖊𝖗𝖊 𝖜𝖎𝖑𝖑 𝖇𝖊 𝖒𝖆𝖘𝖘 𝖊𝖝𝖊𝖈𝖚𝖙𝖎𝖔𝖓𝖘. 𝕿𝖍𝖊 𝕶𝖓𝖎𝖌𝖍𝖙𝖘 𝖔𝖋 𝕭𝖆𝖞𝖊𝖚𝖝.'

Tony choked and gagged. The sight of Stephen Downer's dead and tortured body was too much for him. 'He only left our camp because his dad died,' said Tony, struggling to hold in the tears. 'And they've got everyone else.'

Bob gripped Tony's arm. 'Hold it together, Tony. Focus. If we lose the plot now, it will make our efforts to get them back a lot more difficult.'

They cut Stephen down. His stiff, mutilated body fell into Mickey's arms, and he laid him on the bed.

'What are we going to do with him?' Tony asked. 'He has to have a decent burial.'

'Wrap him in a sheet and put him in the boot,' Bob said. 'There's no point staying here any longer.'

A surge of anger hit Tony. His face tightened, and his teeth gritted. *Bastard. No more apprehension. It's time for action. I want revenge.* 'His family will have two funerals to attend now. It couldn't get any worse, could it?'

The others in the room dropped their heads in respect. For a moment, silence fell across the room.

They carried Stephen's body down the stairs and put him in the boot of Mickey's car. Tony stared at the ground. It was a frosty thing to do with a colleague's corpse, but the only thing they could do. Tears filled his eyes, and he wiped them away.

Tony shrugged his shoulders at Bob. 'Where will we take the body?'

'I have a contact who's an undertaker. He'll get the death registered and has a few trusted registrars who can sort out all the other stuff that goes with it. It's all about greasing the right palms.'

'No doubt you've had to use him in the past then?'

Bob's eyes narrowed as he glared at Tony. 'That's for me to know.'

As they were about to get into Mickey's car, Bob glanced around. 'Did you hear that?' He looked towards the wooded area bordering the house before staring at Tony. 'Someone's calling your name?'

Mickey drew his gun and approached the wooded area. Bob, Tony, and Harry followed. As they drew closer, the source of the sound became clearer.

Tony's chest pounded. 'Uncle Charlie, Is that you?'

SERFDOM AND DISORDER

'I'm over here, behind the oak tree.'

Bob grabbed Tony's arm and gave him a look that urged caution. Tony had already considered that it might be a trap and that his uncle had a gun to his head, but Charlie would never comply if there was a threat. Tony pulled his arm free of Bob's hold and ran towards the dark silhouette of the tree.

On the other side, his uncle sat on the ground. His face was contorted in agony, and there was a large blood stain over his upper leg.

'Charlie! What happened?'

Tony gestured for the other men to help him lift Charlie. Tony crouched at his side. 'I'm so glad you're alive.'

Charlie produced a half smile. 'Yeah, the old boy's still here.'

There was a little laughter at Charlie's response. The four of them lifted him from the ground and carried him to the car.

'No one's carried me like this since my stag night forty-odd years ago.'

Tony smiled. He was the same old Charlie, never letting himself get down about anything. They put him next to the right-hand door in the back of the car. Tony sat in the middle, with Harry on the left-hand side. Mickey took a bandage out of the first aid kit he kept in the glove compartment and fashioned it into a tourniquet.

'Are you going to take me to hospital?'

Bob shook his head. 'We're taking you to a military doctor. He lives in London. Can you tell us what happened?'

Charlie inhaled sharply. 'One minute we were in the house watching TV, and the next thing, two silver vans pulled up. About ten men got out. The men protecting us told us to go upstairs and wait.

'Shots were fired. The door booted open, and they all charged in. I watched it all from the top of the stairs. Our safe-keepers surrendered, and the men came up the stairs. There was a man with them. He looked a right mess. When the Downer family screamed, I realised it was their Stephen. They took him to another room. That's the last we saw of him.

'They forced us all down the stairs, only I lost my footing and slipped. I ended up landing on one of them. Me being the idiot I am, I had a scuffle with the bloke and got shot. They left me on the floor. I thought they would come back for me, but I suppose they thought I would bleed to death.' Charlie grimaced. 'I hope you're going to track these scum down. If you are, I'd love to see their faces when you strike back at them.'

'Uncle Charlie, about Stephen Downer—'

'They killed him, didn't they?'

Tony dropped his head. 'They hanged him.'

'Dirty bastards.'

The car continued towards London, flashing past rows of lighting and trees. There would have been sombre quiet on the journey back if it was just Tony and the three ex-SAS men, but with Charlie present, there would never be deadpan silence. He talked and talked.

Mickey's car reached their first destination, a funeral business. Bob took his phone out and called his friend. The funeral director agreed to take the body. Everyone, apart from Charlie, got out of the car and waited for further instructions.

A man dressed in a white shirt, black tie, and waistcoat came out. 'The side gate's open; just drive through.'

Tony, Harry, and Bob walked through the open metal gate as Mickey returned to the car and reversed it in. The funeral director, Ian Curtis, unlocked a door that led to a plain room: 'Okay, lads, bring the body in here. It's where we embalm them.'

Mickey opened the boot of the car. The four of them carried Stephen Downer inside.

Tony glanced over his shoulder to see if Charlie was okay sitting in the back of the car. His uncle had his face pressed against the back window as if he were observing matters with morbid curiosity.

Inside the building, they unwrapped Stephen's body and placed him on a stainless-steel trolley. Tony turned his head away and clenched his fists as they wheeled Stephen's corpse into cold storage. It was a sad end for a man he was only just getting to know. He had only left the safety of the cabin to comfort his mother. Anyone who loved their family would have done the same, but he'd paid the ultimate price.

They left the funeral parlour and headed back to the car. 'Please tell me you've got a plan of action to get back at these vermin?'

Bob nodded. 'Yeah, I've got a plan. Let's get your uncle's leg treated first. Once that's done, if it's okay with you, Harry, we'll go back to Paddington and discuss what I've got planned.'

Harry nodded in agreement.

22

The bullet in Charlie's right thigh was removed without any complications, much to Tony's relief, and Charlie was now asleep on Harry's sofa.

Although he was happy that his uncle was doing okay, Tony was still worried about Veronica. He tapped his fingers on the tea cup Harry had given him, lost in thought, as he waited for Bob to reveal his plan to free their loved ones.

The other men fixed their attention on Bob as they sat at the kitchen table, drinking tea. Bob seemed to enjoy keeping everyone in suspense, like an actor playing with his audience at a theatre. A wide smile appeared on his face. 'I can see you're all keen on what I have to say next. You're maybe all wondering why I'm smiling.'

No one replied.

Tony's pulse raced. He was desperate to hear some positive news.

'Well, the information I'm about to present to you was out of your way for your own good.'

Tony was about to explode. 'Can you get to the

point, Bob? My woman is being held hostage for fucks sake!'

Bob glared at Tony. 'I gave my wife a tracking device, as a precaution against the situation we're facing now. I checked the device about twenty minutes ago, and I've pinpointed their location.'

'Why didn't you tell us this before? We could have gone in and got them back by now. I've been worried sick.'

Bob's eyes narrowed, and he clenched his fist. 'This isn't the movies. We have to plan these things out and not act on impulse. If we do things off the cuff, we'll endanger everyone.'

Tony acknowledged that Bob was right, but he was frustrated and wanted results now. He took a deep breath. 'You're right. I'm sorry.'

'That's okay, it's understandable. Now, I take it you want to hear the intel and find out where the hostages are?'

The men all nodded.

'They're in an old aircraft hangar in Surrey. I need to go on the internet and do some research – analyse the best method of getting into the hanger. I guarantee it'll be guarded around the perimeter and on the inside too, but my phone isn't much use for research purposes.'

'There's a computer in the spare room and a printer,' Harry said. 'Come on, I'll show you where it is.'

Bob followed Harry out of the kitchen. Tony glanced at Mickey. 'Well that's a relief. At least we know where they are.'

'That was a clever bit of thinking from Bob, giving his wife that device, but that's Bob all over – always one step ahead.'

The kitchen door opened, and Charlie limped inside, grimacing. 'Any chance of a cuppa?'

Tony helped his uncle into one of the spare seats. 'You should be resting.'

'Those bastards have got my Doris. It's a bit hard to rest at a time like this, don't you think? Where's Bob and Harry? What have I missed out on?'

Tony sighed and told him about Bob's revelation about the tracking device.

Charlie relaxed nodded. 'That's great news. I feel a whole lot better now.'

Bob and Harry returned to the kitchen a short time later with a pile of paperwork. They handed a bundle of stapled paper to each person, including Charlie.

Tony hunched forwards as he read through his cluster of paperwork.

Bob gave them a few minutes to read before standing up. 'Right, gentlemen, as you can see from the photos, we got a good look at the hanger from different vantage points. There's an open entrance that allows people to drive in and out and there's a few buildings. The perimeter is fenced off with what appears to be bog-standard barbed-wire fencing. As it turns out, the hanger was a Royal Air Force base until the nineteen eighties. Since then, it's been inactive. Our enemies won't have a clue what's coming.'

Mickey looked up. 'I don't want to piss on your parade, Bob, but what if they found the bugging device? We could be walking into a trap.'

'We'll sound the place out first.'

'Why don't we just exchange hostages?' Tony asked.

'Because it's too complex for there to be an easy outcome. The 1066 group know who we are, apart from Mickey and Harry, of course, and if we exchanged prisoners, that wouldn't be the end of it. We'll always be a threat to these people. They could have us and our families executed at any time they choose.'

Tony sat back, fuming, but agreed with Bob's insight and continued to pay attention.

'We should get some rest,' Bob said. He glanced at his watch. 'It's 0800 now. We'll do a reconnaissance on the aircraft hangar tonight, under the cover of darkness. I'll keep a check on the signal from the tracker until then.'

Tony shook his head. 'What if you get a call for a prisoner exchange before then? We'll be in trouble, won't we?'

Bob smiled. 'I've been in this line of work for a long time now. They won't contact us for a few days yet. These kind of things always drag on. Don't worry, we'll get there. You boys from Civvy Street can sleep in the spare room; there's two beds up there. The SAS boys will take the sleeping bags.'

They all went to their allotted places. Tony was exhausted and couldn't wait to put his head on a pillow to drift off to sleep, but his mind took a little longer to switch off. Images of Veronica being tortured haunted him. *If anything's happened to them, I'll be spitting blood.*

23

Although it was spring with the prospect of warmer weather on the way, it didn't feel very inviting in the darkness of the Surrey countryside. Tony, Bob, Harry, and Mickey were ready to begin their reconnaissance mission in and around the aircraft hangar.

Charlie wasn't with them. He was convalescing after his operation, cared for by Harry's wife and two teenage children. Knowing that his uncle was okay eased Tony's thoughts.

They had dressed in military camouflage, complete with blacked-out faces. They crouched on their approach to the perimeter fence. Bob and Harry carried thick blankets over their arms.

Tony stared at the blanket on Bob's arm. 'What's with the blankets?'

'It's to throw over the barbed wire fence. We'll be able to step over without getting our bollocks tangled then.'

The hangar glowed in the distance like a beacon against the night sky. Tony stared at it and imagined being reunited with Veronica and Aunt Doris.

SERFDOM AND DISORDER

To their surprise, there were no guards by the fence. Bob pulled out his night vision binoculars and scanned the area. 'There're no guards on the perimeter at all. They're not prepared for us, are they?' whispered Bob.

He passed the binoculars to Tony, allowing him to see what Bob deemed lax security measures. He pressed the binoculars against his eyes. It seemed strange seeing everything through night vision. It was dull and bright with glowing green shapes.

The huts near the hanger were old and decrepit; they seemed empty. He glanced around more and noticed two big vans. Farther along, a few figures leaned against a wall. He zoomed in and saw a group of men with automatic weapons, smoking cigarettes. Tony hoped he might see Veronica or one of the others in their group, but there was nothing.

'Come on,' Bob said. 'Let's get closer and look for a way to enter the hangar.'

Bob threw the blanket over the waist-high barbed wire, and they stepped over the fence. Tony and Bob crawled on their stomach towards the hangar. Mickey and Harry ran off in a different direction.

It was tough crawling over sharp stones that cut the palms of their hands. However, the immediate area around the hangar had long grass about five feet tall, which was perfect for doing surveillance work.

Bob and Tony crept close to where the guards stood. Their conversation reminded Tony of his local pub, the Coach and Horses.

'Did you pull that old slapper over the weekend, George?'

The other responded with a laugh. 'Nah, Ron, too

drunk, mate.'

Bob pulled out his binoculars and scanned the area before shuffling close to Tony. 'This will be a piece of cake,' he whispered. 'The hangar's there for the taking.'

'Where's Harry and Mickey?'

'They should be in that hut over there. I'm just waiting for a signal from them, and then we'll create a diversion.'

Tony scowled. 'You never mentioned *that* in the briefing.'

Bob shrugged and returned his attention to the hanger.

Tony didn't like being kept in the dark, but he forced his irritation to the back of his mind. Bob had proven himself time and time again, and now was not the time to doubt him.

They waited for Harry and Mickey to give their signal. Tony heard a loud tapping sound from the area of the derelict hut. The guards drew their guns and looked towards the noise. Tony stared at Bob, waiting for a reaction, uncertain about what to do next.

'Follow me,' Bob said. 'This is where it gets exciting.'

They crawled on the damp, unwelcoming earth towards a jeep that had no guards around it. They got to their feet and onto the grounds of the hangar. Bob stood before the jeep. He produced a small can of petrol from his shoulder bag and poured the flammable liquid under the steering wheel before pulling out a matchbox and striking a match. Bob threw the lit match inside the jeep. Within seconds, flames ignited. Tony and Bob crawled back into the high grass. Bob handed Tony the night vision goggles.

SERFDOM AND DISORDER

The brightness of the fire lit up the black night. The guards turned away from the hut and ran towards the jeep. 'I can smell petrol,' one of them cried out. 'There must be a leak somewhere. I keep telling you to stub your cigarettes out!'

Tony saw Harry and Mickey running towards the hangar. Mickey had a camera around his neck. He stood in various positions and took photos.

The guards outside alerted others about the blazing jeep, and four more men ran out of the hanger. One of them held a fire extinguisher. Soon, the fire faded. Arguments broke out amongst the guards about how the fire had started. Harry and Mickey sprinted back towards the hut and laid low.

Tony raised a triumphant thumb to Bob. Within fifteen minutes of the fire being put out, the guards returned to their lax indifference, believing the fire was down to a petrol leak.

Bob and Tony headed back to the perimeter fence where they had first entered. They waited just inside it for Harry and Mickey, but time seemed to drag with no sign of them.

Come on, you two, what the fuck is keeping you? The coast's well clear!

Mickey and Harry appeared in his vision, and Tony gave Bob another thumbs up. Tony was pleased no one had needed to fire a shot. He had been worried about their people getting hurt in a fire fight.

'Come on, you two. You're getting old,' Bob teased as the other two ran towards them.

They climbed back over the perimeter fence and headed to the van. Everyone was in good spirits, having completed a successful reconnaissance with no incident.

Heavy rain descended as they drove away from the hangar, impacting on the windows. The windscreen wiper moved at rapid speed but didn't do much to help their visibility.

'We timed that well, didn't we? A few minutes later and we would have got drenched,' said Bob, rubbing his hands together.

Harry laughed. 'Look at the mess we're in, covered in shit and messing the van up. Hate to say it, but we need to stand in that downpour and wash the grease off our faces. If the police drive past and notice us, we're fucked.'

They stood in the pouring rain, rubbing their hands over their hands and faces. Grease paint got into Tony's mouth, and he coughed. He couldn't wait to get back to London and have a proper shower – a hot shower – and a hot cup of tea, with a heavy dose of sleep thrown in for good measure.

24

On the journey back from Surrey, Tony pestered Mickey about the photos he had taken around the hanger. He wanted any information he could get about their families and friends. Any photo from the hangar of Veronica or Doris would have calmed him. The lack of information pissed him off, and he let off a loud sigh.

Mickey wouldn't reveal anything. He insisted on sharing the images with Bob first. Once they had devised a plan, he told Tony he'd be free to analyse the snaps.

That night, Tony tossed and turned in his bed. He stared up at the ceiling. The insomnia he was suffering had nothing to do with the sleeping facilities; his mind just wouldn't rest. He wanted to go back to the hangar now and free everyone.

Rolling around in bed was a drag and he felt the urge to get up and make himself a cup of tea, but wandering around a stranger's house made him feel uneasy. He put the pillow over his face, cursed, then punched the mattress.

He kept glancing at the watch he'd left on the small

bedside table. The mission was everything to him, so much depended on it.

From nowhere, the lights that had been troubling Tony surrounded him. He found himself back in the tunnel with the bright glowing light at the end of it. Panic overcame him; he yelped as a soft voice entered his head. 'Tony, you must stop panicking. You will be wiser when the time is right.'

The bright lights and tunnel faded away. Tony's vision readjusted, and he found himself in an unfamiliar room. Tony grimaced and narrowed his eyes. He twisted and turned on his seat, not knowing how he got there.

'What's going on with you?' Bob asked. 'Have you got a vibrator up your arse or something?'

Laughter rang around the room.

Tony forced a grin, realising that time had shifted forward once again. *Whoever created that tunnel, thank you for your time-moving skills.*

His focus returned, and he stared at the presentation of photos Mickey had taken at the hanger. Bob stood at the side of the large screen, offering insights and observations.

'The first photo shows the entrance door, positioned on the far side of the hangar. The front was bricked up, as it's not officially in use anymore. Lucky for us, it's on the same side as the derelict huts. If it had been on the other side, it would have made matters more difficult.'

Photos two and three came next. They didn't offer Tony the reassurance he craved, but when the fourth photo appeared, he froze. There was a gap in the hangar's structure, about three-feet wide, and through it, he saw Doris and Veronica. They were standing together in what looked like conversation. The other hostages surrounded them, along with three armed guards, placed at a distance.

Other photos revealed that the prisoners slept in metal bunk beds, congregated close to each other. There were images of the other men's families and the other half of their team.

The images of Richard, Simon, John, and Jim were crystal clear. Everyone could see how bruised and beaten they all were, and it gave each of them food for thought.

A jolt of sickness flooded Tony's body. It was unnerving to see his team in such a state. He cursed and swore.

The briefing ended, and Bob switched the lights back on. Tony still didn't have a clue where he was, but that didn't matter.

'We've got all the information we need for now,' Bob said. 'We know what part of the hangar our families and brothers in arms are in, so we're going to split into two groups again. It's obvious what we've got to do once we're inside the hangar. Just make the attacks quick and deadly. I'm going to call in some favours and get a couple of vans and drivers.'

Tony smiled. 'Do we have two people we can trust for the driving jobs? Oh, sorry, I forgot myself there. We are, after all, dealing with Bob Davis. You've no doubt got contacts in mind.'

'I have two people I can trust, yes. If that's okay with you, sarcastic bollocks?'

Tony nodded. Tonight was make-or-break time. It was vital that Bob's plan paid off. The alternative didn't bear thinking about.

For Tony, just a glimpse of Veronica had made him realise how much he loved her. He glanced at the silver clock; the time read eight thirty. 'When are we leaving, Bob?'

'About midnight, but until then, we need to arrange what weapons we're taking and get ourselves changed into combat fatigues.'

Once the weapons were allocated and they had changed, they returned to the briefing room. Tony was dressed in his battle clothes and was ready to go. He glanced at his reflection in the window, feeling justified wearing an army uniform. *This is for a good cause. No one likes violence, unless it's required.*

Bob, together with Mickey, were loaded with four SR-762 auto-loaded rifles, as well as the pistols they had carried with them on the visit to Fairplay House. They carried a few grenades with them for good measure.

Tony was deep in thought. His earlier enthusiasm had dwindled. The clock on the wall, with its continuous clicks seemed slower and louder than usual, and it irritated him. He scratched his head and kept looking around the room, even though there was nothing to look at. He repeatedly looked at the clock and checked it against his own watch, counting down the hours and minutes. It was still only eleven. They had another hour to go before they headed off.

A doorbell rang out, snapping Tony out of his thoughts. Bob got out of his chair and opened the door, then ran down a set of stairs. Tony heard another door opening and Bob offering friendly greetings to whoever had rung the bell.

Tony glanced at Harry, who had finished stripping his rifle bare, and shrugged his shoulders.

Harry laughed. 'It's the prostitutes you captured from the raids.'

'What! At a time like this? What the fuck—'

Harry laughed out loud. 'Blimey, you're real easy to wind up, ain't ya? It's the drivers for the mission tonight, you idiot.'

'For a moment there, I believed you.'

'Yeah. If I had my phone nearby, I'd have taken a photo of your reaction.'

The two drivers entered and nodded to everyone in the room. Bob introduced them, 'Gentlemen, I worked with both these men in the Forces. They served in the Parachute Regiment. This is Paul,' he said tapping the man to his left, 'and this is Cliff.'

Paul and Cliff had stern, serious faces. They both sported a short-cropped haircut and narrow eyes and mouths. They must have been at least six-foot-two.

Bob handed them both a Beretta 92 handgun and back-up magazines. They gave their pistols a thorough examination; no one distracted them. They were professional men doing their job. After the pistols passed their stringent examination, Cliff spoke in what sounded like a South Wales accent. 'I'll be picking you all up when the mission's complete, together with the rest of your men.'

'I'll be transporting the civilians to a safe zone,' Paul said in a Teesside accent, 'and I won't be hanging around for anyone.'

'That's reassuring to hear. We can't have innocent people getting caught in the crossfire,' said Tony.

Everyone nodded.

At midnight, they rose from their chairs and shook each other's hands in a gesture of togetherness and to wish each other good luck. Two white Fiat Ducato vans waited outside. Bob, Tony, and Cliff got into one van, while Harry, Mickey, and Paul got in the other. A host of ammunition was loaded into both vans under the cover of large bags.

Tony glanced around, still trying to work out where he was. It looked like the grounds of an industrial estate. Not far off, he saw a sign that read West London Industrial Village, Chiswick, W4.

They weren't too far away from Surrey then. He sighed. At least they weren't on the other side of London.

The vans drove out of the industrial estate together, heading towards the old aircraft hangar. Tony experienced a sudden surge of energy. He wanted to kill everyone holding their people hostage.

SERFDOM AND DISORDER

25

The two vans arrived at the outskirts of the old aircraft hangar. Each member of the team looked pumped up for action. In addition to having a handgun each, Bob gave Cliff and Paul a hand grenade, just in case it was needed.

Bob spoke to Cliff and Paul. 'Don't forget, lads, when I set off the flare, that's the cue for you both to drive up to the hangar.'

Orders were given, and weapons were checked. The team was ready to embark on a do-or-die mission. Mickey handed around dark face paint. They looked illusive and intimidating.

Bob and Tony ran towards the eastern side of the hangar, while Mickey and Harry headed to the west. Tony glared at the glow of the hangar, as if entranced by its presence as he had been on their first visit.

They were back to crawling on their stomach across grassland, moving along it like two reptiles looking for food. It was a perfect place for cover.

Tony was trying to hold it together, but his breathing became erratic. He understood that if he flipped his mind, their position could be jeopardised and the hostages executed. He focused on clearing his mind and controlling his breathing.

Bob had his night vision goggles glued to his face. 'Mickey and Harry have made it to the hut,' he informed Tony. 'Come on.'

They crawled closer to the hangar. The two guards outside the front were chatting and smoking cigarettes, oblivious to what was going on around them.

Bob whispered into Tony's ear. 'I'll throw a stone in their direction. It'll distract them from our position. Harry and Mickey will be watching from the hut. If everything has gone to plan, they'll sneak into the hangar. We'll follow them inside. Then it'll be down to luck whether we can pull this mission off.'

Tony gripped his pistol. He closed his eyes for a moment and offered a brief prayer, even though he had no religious inclinations.

Bob stared at the large stone in the palm of his hand, kissed it, and tossed it over the guard's heads. They turned their backs on Bob and Tony as they got up to investigate the noise. Bob and Tony leapt from their cover and ran towards their targets. One of the guards spun around, but Bob took him out before the guard had even raised his gun and then shot the second guard. Both guards fell to the ground and laid in lifeless limbo.

Tony glanced at the guards' corpses, and his heart pounded at a furious rate. A bead of sweat ran down his forehead, and he wiped it. He stared at his hand that held his weapon, it was steady. Nerves hadn't got the better of him.

Harry and Mickey sprinted out of the hut and headed

for the side door of the hangar. Bob nodded at Tony and he followed closely behind, their footsteps splashing on damp and soggy ground.

Gunfire rang out the moment they entered the hangar. They dove behind some metallic cases and rusting forklift trucks and fired back. Bob signaled for the hostages to lie on the floor, and some of the women screamed.

The shots continued to ring out as the hostage-takers edged forward. The sound of bullets impacting walls and ricocheting in all directions made Tony flinch. He looked at Bob for guidance, but all he saw was Bob firing back.

Tony followed Bob's stance and began to fire at the targets approaching him. His brain scattered into a multitude of directions, as he focused on the people he cared about, getting out of the hanger alive, and hitting the targets in front of him.

More bullets whizzed past Tony. He wanted to break cover and charge forward; the desperation to end the situation became a chronic need. He needed composure, he needed focus. This wasn't a time to become erratic.

Having cover to hide behind whilst shooting open targets could only go one way. One by one, the targets before Tony fell to the ground in a crescendo of bullets. The sounds of sobs coming from some of the hostages could be heard between the hallow of gun fire.

The raid had caught the hostage-takers off-guard. Being in an open aircraft hanger gave those who carried out the invasion total advantage. Tony breathed a short breath of relief, but it didn't last long. Some shouting rang out. Tony looked and noticed a startled member of the enemy, swaying unsteadily on his feet. His breath was uneven; he swore at all around him. Desperation flowed out of his every pore.

The man leaned forward and picked up Veronica, dragging her from the floor. He stood behind her with his forearm around her throat. 'One wrong move and she gets it. Back off and let me go.'

Tony's mouth slackened, and he shook his head. His gun arm shook as his mind raced through every possible way of resolving the situation without Veronica getting harmed.

Bob put a hand on Tony's arm as he called out. 'We'll let you go, no problem. But on one condition.'

'What's that, then?'

'That you don't touch a hair on that woman's head. If you do, you know the consequences.'

'Don't piss me about. Just get me the fuck out of here.'

'Walk towards the exit with your hostage and keep walking until you're feeling safe. Once you reached a distance you would call secure, let her go.'

Bob kept his hand on Tony's shoulder as he continued to speak in a soft, reassuring tone. 'Come on, then, get moving.'

'I don't want no funny stuff. Just let me go, and she'll be fine.'

'Yeah, sure, that's no problem.'

The guard walked backwards towards the door. He removed his arm from her throat and pulled her by her dress. Her body trembled, as did her lips and chin. In the split second the guard turned his head away, Bob fired at him, hitting him in the throat. He fell to the floor choking and gagging as blood pumped out of him. Within seconds, he was dead.

Veronica ran to Tony and hugged him. Her trembling continued as she sobbed hard into his chest.

Bob broke them apart. 'Okay, it's great to see each other, but the ordeal is over. Let's get moving.'

The mission had been a success. There were brief hugs and kisses and tears of relief, but they weren't safe until they were far away.

Bob pulled the flare gun out of his backpack and headed outside, gesturing for Tony and Veronica to follow him. He pointed the gun skyward and pulled the trigger. There was a swishing noise, and the sky lit up a beautiful red glow.

Within a matter of minutes, the two vans sped towards the hangar. Bob and Tony remained outside to greet the vans as the happy reunions continued inside.

Cliff turned the van and reversed it at speed to the nearest exit point of the hangar. The backdoors opened, and Richard, John, Simon, and Jim jumped into the van. The civilians climbed into the larger, second vehicle. Tony pried Veronica from his arms with a promise that he would see her again soon. Once they were sure everyone was present, Bob slammed the backdoor shut and knocked on the roof to signal Paul to get the van moving. They sped away.

Tony watched the van go. Bob shook his shoulder. 'Come on, Tony. Time to go.'

Tony got into the back of Cliff's van and sat on the

floor. He glanced up at his friends from the cabin. Their faces were bruised, bloodied, and swollen, yet their eyes sparkled with joy.

Simon nodded. 'Thanks, lads. You don't know what we went through in that place. It was brutal.'

'I could handle getting boozed tonight, that's for sure,' Richard said.

Bob grinned. 'Let's all calm down and get everybody back to the safe house first.'

Tony shrugged his shoulders towards Bob. 'Where is this safe house anyway?'

'It's a farmhouse in Kent. We're renting it from the local estate agents. Recently refurbished and decorated.'

Thoughts of Veronica dominated Tony's mind. He had a positive glow inside now, but for a while back there, he had been convinced she would be killed. He glanced at Bob. 'I can't thank you enough for what you did back there. You saved Veronica's life. I'm at your service forever.'

Bob smiled. 'Well, I might have to take advantage of that; you can become my personal slave. You can polish my shoes, make me breakfast, hell, you can even wipe my arse if you like.' Everyone in the van laughed, Tony included.

'Wiping your arse will be a pleasure. If you've got any spare sandpaper, it would do the perfect job.'

The journey from Surrey to Kent passed quickly, and they were soon pulling into a driveway outside a large house. The other van had arrived before them, but nobody had gone inside yet. Everyone stood congregated in one large group outside the front door. They all looked tired and in need of a good night's sleep.

SERFDOM AND DISORDER

It was still dark, so it was difficult to see the farmhouse in all its glory, but it looked huge. It had to be to have room for everyone.

Mickey led the group towards the farmhouse. 'You want to see inside – the landlord has had the place all done up.'

The door opened, and the smell of paint hit Tony. Mickey turned on the lights. The walls were pastel, complementing the varnished wood floors.

Everyone had a look of awe on their faces. The farmhouse had been transformed into multi-personal living quarters. There were rooms along one corridor with more up the stairs, and each room was fitted with a personal bathroom. The kitchen was spotless and gleamed, complete with a new cooker. The communal living room had a huge screen TV, together with cosy sofas and armchairs. It was a perfect space to hide away in.

Tony was shown to a room with a double bed, a wardrobe, and a chest of drawers, not that they had any luggage to unpack. Veronica sat on the bed and patted the space behind her. Tony obliged her request. They kissed and caressed, only to be disturbed by a knock on the door.

Tony laughed and felt antagonised at the same time. 'I can't win, can I?'

It was Bob, and he had a huge grin on his face. 'Come on, lover boy. We're having a meeting in the kitchen. Tell Veronica the others civvies are in the living room. Don't let her sit in here on her own.'

'Just as I was relaxing, you had to come along and spoil it all.'

Bob shrugged. Tony shut the door and returned to Veronica. 'I've got a meeting to attend in the kitchen. Everyone else is in the living room area if you want to go and see them.'

He escorted Veronica to the living room and then headed to the kitchen, curious about Bob's plan for the next mission. The other men were already seated around the kitchen table, surrounded by glossy new work tables and fresh white wall tiles. Beer cans scattered around the table. Tony gazed at his battered-looking friends. He felt a tinge of sadness for what they must have gone through. At the same time, he felt guilty for getting away from the assault in the cabin, though if he and Bob hadn't, there would have been no one left to rescue them.

Bob didn't waste any time getting started. 'Before I go any further, I'd like to welcome you all back. I'm sorry we couldn't get to you sooner.'

Richard took a big swig from his can of beer and gulped it down. Both his eyes were bruised, and his nose was twisted; he looked a sorry sight. 'They beat us – every day – in front of our families. They wanted information about our movement and our plans. We had it bad, but nowhere as bad as Stephen. Sick bastards told us how they'd tortured him for a confession.'

Everyone nodded.

Richard took another gulp of his beer. 'I wasn't far from confessing myself, but I was afraid they would execute everyone.'

Bob walked up to Richard and squeezed his shoulder. 'You should all be proud of yourselves. They put you through hell, and you kept your mouth shut. That's commendable, and you have my utmost respect – all of you.'

Tony raised his can and proposed a toast. 'To those who pulled through the ordeal. You saved this movement from collapse. Cheers.'

Bob, Micky, and Harry joined him in the toast, raising their cans in the air with a cheer.

'And to a father and son team,' Bob said, raising his can again. 'The Downers. May you both rest in peace.'

This time the word 'cheers' rang around the table, though they all looked sombre as they offered a memory to two innocent, law-abiding people trying to expose the evil happening in Britain.

'Okay, men,' Bob said. 'We have to focus on the goals this movement set out to achieve. We have to continue the momentum and strike back at the 1066 group and Murphy. We've deprived them of a few brothels and some officials and taken some of their cash, but we need to do more.' He glanced at each of the men in turn. 'I say we strike them where it hurts. First, we find out where Murphy drinks. Second, we raid the 1066 club and shoot to kill the lot of them. If there's one group that should exhibit no mercy, it's ours. Now, if anyone wants to drop out, I'll understand. I won't hold it against you.'

Richard crushed his empty lager can. 'Are you saying that after what we've been through that we're not up to the job? How can we have any objections? We want revenge!'

The other men nodded their agreement, and an awkward silence fell across the table. Tony stood up and went to the fridge, grabbing a can of lager for each of the men. When he returned to the table, he shoved a can into each man's hands.

'I'm in,' Tony said as he resumed his seat. 'But I think we need some time to wind down and calm down. There's no need for any animosity between us. Bob's not saying we're not good enough. He's giving us a chance to walk away, if that's what we want.'

Richard nodded and pulled the ring pull on his can. 'You're right. Sorry, Bob. I guess I'm not thinking straight.'

Bob glanced around the table. 'Shall we have a vote on it? All those in favour of winding down for the night, say aye.'

'Aye.' The decision was unanimous; further plans would have to wait.

26

The next day following the drinking session, Tony sat upright in his cosy new bed with Veronica, his arm draped around her shoulder. Tony's head was as heavy as an anvil. His body wasn't all that great a condition either. 'Why do I keep doing that? I keep telling myself not to overdo the alcohol.'

Veronica grinned. 'Maybe you should listen to your own advice.'

'And where's the fun in that?'

By the time late afternoon came around, the effects of the hangover had subsided, and he reported to the kitchen with the rest of the team.

As usual, Bob stood at the head of the table ready to begin his briefing. 'I want to finish the job of killing Murphy. Take him out of the equation. I know where he drinks.'

'So where does that bastard drink?' John asked.

'All around his manor, in places where no one will cause him any trouble.'

'That's not an answer!'

'The Telegraph – in Stratford. Murphy goes there

on a Wednesday afternoon, buys a few locals a drink, and plays darts for a few hours. Murphy and his thugs play for money. No one bothers him for obvious reasons.'

Tony sat up straight. 'I know that pub! It's not far from me – but a Wednesday afternoon? I didn't think you'd get many people drinking at that time of day.'

'There's a little drinking club that goes in there during the week. I've been told it can get quite packed.' He shrugged. 'It seems odd, but there you go.'

Tony reasoned about the tribal mindset. It made sense now he thought about it. 'Do you think he'll notice us? We'd be new faces, so to speak. We'd stand out, wouldn't we?'

'Not if it's packed, but we'll just have to take our chances.'

Tony nodded and thought back to Veronica. He had gotten her back but felt further away from her than ever. He yearned to spend more time with her and he would, once they'd sorted out Murphy and the 1066 group. *Just wish I could retire to bed and sleep it off with Veronica at my side all day.*

'Are you okay there, Tony? You look like you're in a trance,' John asked.

'Yeah, everything's fine. Thanks, John. The drink gives me a hard time the day after a session.'

They agreed to attack the Telegraph in three days' time. Until then, they would lay low at the farmhouse. They had more than enough provisions to keep everyone comfortable.

Once the meeting was over, Tony went to see Charlie, who'd arrived a few hours earlier. He was glad to see his uncle had recovered from the operation to remove the bullet from his leg, and patted him on the shoulder.

'Hello, Charlie, it's good to see you up and about. I was worried about you, but you look great.'

'Cheers, son. I feel great, thanks to Harry's wife and kids. They made sure I was well looked after. In fact, I got treated like royalty.'

They spoke for a few minutes more about trivial matters; it was a welcome diversion from more serious issues.

The next few days and nights passed quickly, with each person doing their bit to make it a pleasant stay. Someone – probably Bob – had even secured clean clothes and toiletries for everyone, and there was an air of community spirit.

For Tony, the cosy environment made him all the more aware that he was too soft. He loved being with Veronica, but war was around the corner and he needed to toughen up.

Wednesday came far too quickly. Tony awoke to the touch of soft sheets wrapped around him and Veronica's warm, smooth body. He turned off the alarm clock; it was seven thirty. Tony groaned. He wanted to remain in bed, but he had to focus on the challenge in front of him. The situation demanded nothing less.

He stared at Veronica as she lay sleeping beside him. She was so beautiful, so perfect. The love he had for her was beyond words. He kissed her forehead. She felt so enticing, so welcoming. It was a wrench to leave her, but he forced himself out of bed and got dressed. He kissed Veronica again before heading to the kitchen.

J.P. GADSTON

All the team had congregated together. Bob stood away from the table, an intense gaze on each of the men in turn, as if assessing their readiness.

'Before we begin,' Bob said, 'they'll be a few of you who won't like this. Those of you held captive got your faces marked up, and it'll make you all stand out. In a place like the Telegraph, that's going to be a problem. It'll look suspect and draw attention to us. Anyone disagree?'

No one said a word.

'Well, that's great because I have two ladies that my wife is friends with who work as makeup artists in the film industry. They're going to come in and cover up all of those blemishes and bruises.'

As if on cue, two women in their mid-to-late thirties entered the kitchen. Bob introduced them. 'The lady on my left is Rachel, and the lady on my right is Diane.'

The men said their hellos, and one by one, each of the men had their bruises skillfully covered up. The ladies did a professional job; each man underwent a complete transformation.

The ladies packed their equipment into bags, said their goodbyes, and departed. Bob nodded his approval. 'We'll go to London in one van, which I'll be driving. Once we're there, we'll split into two groups again. I assume you've all got your handguns and ammo?'

Everyone nodded.

'I want the four of us who liberated the aircraft hangar close to the tables near the dartboard – that's where Murphy and his men will be. The other four I want positioned on the other side of the pub. When I give the nod, those on the far side of the bar will harass people and drive them out. Murphy will conclude that trouble's brewing, but before they have a chance to do anything, Murphy and his entourage will get executed. Then, we leave the pub and go on our own sweet way.'

They departed from the kitchen and walked out to the smaller of the Fiat vans. They had all dressed casually, in a shirt or polo shirt, jeans, and trainers or shoes. It was vital they didn't stand out.

Tony took the passenger seat next to the driver. The rest of them piled into the back.

As the van began its journey to London, the scenery helped Tony focus on keeping calm. He didn't want to engage in too much small talk, but as he was sitting next to Bob, he would probably be involved in the conversation whether he wanted to or not.

The usual pop music played in the background. It seemed that music from the sixties, seventies, and eighties were a favourite of Bob's. Together with the scenery, it made a welcome distraction to what lay before him.

Bob appeared relaxed behind the wheel. He sang along to some of the songs. His voice was irritating and annoying, but also amusing.

'You like the sound of your voice, don't you, Bob?'

Bob smiled. 'Do I detect a hint of jealousy in your observation, Mr Harrison? I can't help it if my vocal achievements don't meet your seal of approval.'

'I can't believe how at ease you are. We're about to go on a deadly mission, and you're singing without a care in the world.'

'It's just another mission. You learn how to cope with extreme emotions eventually. I'm used to it.'

The van continued towards Stratford. The closer they got, the more pumped up Tony felt, and he kept fidgeting with his pistol.

On the borders of Stratford and Plaistow, Bob pulled the van down a quiet side road. Apart from some grannies chatting on the street corner, there wasn't anyone about.

Bob parked the van and turned off the engine. The men got out and stretched their legs. There were the usual yawns and groans that accompanied a long journey. They didn't look anything like a fighting force. More like a load of blokes going out on a drinking session.

'The pub's just up the road,' Bob said to Simon, Richard, John, and Jim. 'Walk up to the top of the road, then turn left and keep on walking. Remember, I want you on the other side of the pub, away from Murphy. I'll give you twenty minutes to get yourselves settled. Then me, Tony, Harry, and Mickey will enter. If there's any trouble before we arrive, text me. We'll move quicker if that scenario happens. This is our chance to take out Murphy for good. Let's not blow it.'

The first half of their party wandered off. Tony watched them walk up the road and disappear around the corner. He couldn't help thinking back to the last time he had seen Murphy and the attack on Stephen's dad. He glanced at his watch. Time had been standing still, but it was now time to get things moving. The twenty-minute wait was up.

'They haven't contacted us, so I assume everything's fine,' said Tony, looking to the other men for reassurance.

SERFDOM AND DISORDER

Mickey laughed. 'Yeah, let's hope they haven't been shot.'

Harry kept the dark humour going, aiming it at Tony. 'I expect they've got themselves tortured in the toilets by now.'

'How can you joke about this? I want to get in the pub and sort that bastard out.'

Micky, Harry, and Bob roared with laughter. They didn't seem to have a care in the world. Bob patted Tony on the back. 'It'll be fine, Tony. Just keep yourself calm.'

The four of them got back in the van for the short journey to the Telegraph. Tony envisioned himself shooting Murphy and his henchmen. He clutched the underside of the seat and breathed hard.

Bob gave him a quick sideways glance. 'What's got into you? You'd better not act like this in the pub. You'll draw attention to us.'

'Once I've had a beer, I should be okay.'

'Just keep calm. We fight when it's time to fight.'

Tony nodded.

Bob steered the van into the car park. The Telegraph was a detached building surrounded by a tower block, rows of houses, and three-storey maisonettes. Built in the mid-nineteen sixties, together with the housing stock, the Telegraph had seen its fair share of violence over the years.

Bob and Tony got out of the van and looked around, then opened the back door of the van so Mickey and Harry could get out.

'Right, men,' Bob said. 'Now's the time to do the business. Are you all ready?'

They all nodded. As they drew nearer to the pub, Tony could see through the windows that the place was full. He hoped Murphy would recognise him from the Libra Arms; he wanted to shoot the scumbag.

Harry led the way through the main entrance with his head held high and shoulders upright. A crescendo of noise greeted them – drunken laughter, the chime of slot machines, and eighties pop music at full pelt. It was mostly full of men, with only a few women here and there.

Tony had a quick glance at the left side of the pub. Murphy looked suave and smooth in his grey suit, white shirt, and red silk tie. He was playing darts with five other men, also dressed in suits. They all looked drunk and were shouting at one another.

Harry was the first to get a drink. The bar area was so full of people trying to get served that it became a mission in itself. 'You'd think it was a Friday night,' he yelled to Bob over the noise.

Bob, standing near the bar, nodded in agreement and gave off his customary smile as Harry handed over four beers. Tony took a large swig from his pint. There was nowhere to sit, so they stayed where they were, not too far from Murphy. Tony had a fleeting look around the pub to see where the others were. He spotted them at the far end, in their designated area. Richard glanced at Tony for a brief second and then turned his attention elsewhere.

An hour had passed, in which time they had each consumed three pints of lager. Tony was beginning to feel a little drunk, but more than ready for the challenge before him. He glared at Murphy with narrowed eyes.

SERFDOM AND DISORDER

Bob nodded to the men on the other side of the pub, giving them the signal to get in position.

Murphy shouted amongst the din. 'I've seen you before, ain't I?'

'Have you?' Tony asked, forcing himself to remain calm.

'Yeah… you're the bloke that was outside the Libra Arms that night. That was you, weren't it?'

Murphy placed his left hand inside his suit pocket, pulled out a cut-throat razor, and flicked it open. Everyone around Murphy backed away, but they stayed close enough to watch events unravel.

Tony threw his pint glass at Murphy's face. Having a team of ex-SAS men at his side gave him the confidence he needed to face Murphy himself. He did it for Stephen, for Stephen's dad, and Veronica. But most of all, he did it for everyone whose lives would be destroyed by the drugs he was peddling. The glass hit its target. Blood streamed down Murphy's face.

A woman screamed, and the background music stopped. Innocent bystanders rushed for the exit. The pub emptied within a matter of minutes.

A mass brawl broke out between Murphy's men and Bob's team. Bar stools were picked up and thrown. and tables tossed. Glasses and bottles flew then smashed on the floor.

Murphy's men each pulled out a knife and charged forward with sneers full of contempt.

Bob pulled out his pistol, and the rest of the team followed suit, but it was too late. Murphy's men attacked, swinging and jabbing their blades. Bob sidestepped and kicked the man nearest to him in the bollocks. The attacker dropped to the floor, his face contorted in agony. Bob stamped on his throat, instantly killing him.

Pete Foster, the man who had knocked on his door and threatened him, landed a punch flush on Tony's jaw. A sharp pain shot through his head and down his back. His legs wobbled, and he fell into a table.

Foster gripped Tony's throat, cutting off his air supply. As he started to choke, he groped around the table for something he could use as a weapon and grabbed a bottle. Tony smashed it over Foster's head, causing the man's scalp to gush blood. Using the jagged edge of the bottle, he stabbed Foster in the face and neck. Blood sprayed, and Foster fell to the floor.

The team from the other side of the pub fired their weapons, and one by one, Murphy's men fell to the floor.

Murphy dived over the counter and exited through the back door.

Bob looked at Tony. 'He's fucked off round the back. Come on.'

Tony and Bob ran out of the pub. Murphy was running in zig-zags, bumping into parked cars as he looked behind him, before crouching behind a parked car. 'Come any closer and you'll fucking get it. Now, back off.'

Bob tugged Tony's shoulder. 'I'll go to the left, you to the right. Approach him from behind.'

Tony nodded. He inched forward using the cars as a shield.

'You fucking pricks better keep out of my way,' Murphy shouted. 'You come into my manor taking

SERFDOM AND DISORDER

liberties... I'll kill you – and your families.'

A shot rang out, hitting the window of the car Tony hid behind. Glass showered over his head. He cursed Murphy under his breath.

'You don't enter my manor and give it the big bollocks to me. I run this place.'

Murphy fired another shot, but it didn't hit any apparent target.

Bob signaled to him. 'You ready, Tony? Let's do it.'

They stood up and charged forward, firing rounds of bullets through the car Murphy was hiding behind.

When they reached him, Murphy was lying on the floor, his eyes glazed and vacant, blood trickled from his mouth. When he spoke, his tone was feeble and strained. 'Come on, lads, we don't need to fight. We can talk about all this. If you want money, I've got plenty. Just say the word, and your bank accounts will be bulging.'

Tony and Bob looked at each other, nodded, and then turned back to Murphy. They both raised their pistols and fired. Murphy's body jolted. He was dead, finally.

Bob nodded at Tony. 'Let's get back to the boozer.'

Upon entering the pub, the other members of the team aimed their weapons at Bob and Tony, ready to shoot, but put them down again.

Mickey grinned. 'Shall we go, then?'

The pub looked like it had been hit by a bomb blast. Bar stools, tables, and chairs were broken. There was smashed glass everywhere. Dead bodies were scattered. It wasn't pleasant viewing.

They put away their guns and returned to the van.

Tony's heart pounded. He was high on adrenaline but had mixed feelings about killing Murphy. He had deserved what was coming to him, but that didn't make killing right.

The car park was vacant, but sirens approached. All eight men climbed into the van, and Bob sped away. Pop music blared, filling what would have otherwise been an uncomfortable silence.

Bob gave Tony a quick glance. 'You're buzzing now, ain't ya? On a massive high?'

'I don't know what I am, to be honest.'

Bob smiled and turned up the radio. 'The only thing pissing me off is that we had to leave the pub. I was just getting a taste for the booze. Perhaps we can make up for it when we get back to the farmhouse.'

Tony smiled, just as his vision blurred again. He jolted forward as the man in the black jumpsuit appeared before him, almost as if he were floating outside the windscreen.

'Are you okay, Tony?' Bob asked. 'You jumped halfway out your chair.'

'I'm on a rush. I can't describe it, mate.'

The man in the black jumpsuit spoke. As usual, it was only Tony who could hear him, making him believe he really was ready for a straightjacket.

'Tony you've achieved an historic feat today. You're a hero. We look forward to seeing you again soon.' The man evaporated.

Tony was bewildered. *An historic feat? What the fuck was all that about?*

Tony wanted to switch off and go to sleep, but the adrenaline rushing through his body and mind wouldn't allow that. He rested his head against the window instead, staring at the road ahead.

They pulled into the drive of the farmhouse just over an hour later. Tony still felt numb. They had done it. They had taken out Shaun Murphy, the biggest and most revered thug in East London. The amazing thing about it was how easy it had all been.

27

Two weeks passed since the killings at the Telegraph, during which time, everyone involved had laid low with their families. The killings had attracted massive media attention. Every genre of media reported on it. The tabloids sensationalised the event, predicting a gang war in the near future, while the more up-market press criticized how lawless working-class Britain had become.

Everyone followed the media's over-reaction with a dry smile. Bob called a meeting in the kitchen, though he had since renamed it the bunker as its name had connotations with its place as a centre of operations.

Bob stood at the end of the kitchen table with his arms crossed as he always did, ready to address the others as they sat around the table drinking their usual cups of tea and coffee. 'The media haven't a clue about the killings at the Telegraph. They make up a load of old garbage to keep everyone interested.'

'That's the idea,' Tony said. 'It's got nothing to do with the news or facts; it's about distorting events so they have something exciting and print-worthy.'

SERFDOM AND DISORDER

Richard took a sip of his coffee. 'Do you believe if the truth came out about Murphy's execution, the media would report on it?'

Harry shook his head. 'The security services would give the story a news blackout. Information like that would bring down governments.'

John looked irked. 'Bring down governments? And the rest! It would bring down the whole establishment. But what a revelation it would be. The public would finally realise they're being governed by a load of crooked manipulators.'

Simon stretched his arms outward and yawned. 'I'll bet the Home Office and the Met cooked up the story about what happened at the Telegraph. Then fed it to the media.'

The debate continued as passions arose about the way the media manipulated facts. Whether or not they had an awareness of the truth regarding the matter was anyone's guess.

Bob brought the debate to an end. There were more pressing matters to discuss, namely plans for their next mission against the 1066 group. 'Murphy was just one chink amongst many in the 1066 group's armour. Now that chink has gone, we can move onto our next manoeuvre. We've still got our bargaining chips at the table: the officials we've kept hostage.'

Tony raised his hand.

'Yes, Tony, what's up?'

'Correct me if I'm wrong, but has anyone heard any news reports about the people we took captive? Have they been reported as missing?'

It appeared that no one had checked. There were a

lot of murmurs and puzzled facial expressions.

'You would have thought these people disappearing would have been headline news,' Tony continued. 'More so with the missing politicians.'

Simon offered his journalistic opinion. 'The security services must be covering it up. They'll have briefed the families and friends, probably with threats and lies to stop anyone reporting it to the media.'

Mickey leaned forward. 'So what is the plan for the prisoners, Bob?'

'We're going to interrogate the ones who are members of the 1066 group. I want to know when their next big event is, the one with human sacrifices.'

John frowned. 'Can we believe what they tell us? They'll say anything at this point, won't they?'

'We'll tell them we know where their families are and what will happen to them if they lie to us. If their stories corroborate, then it should be the truth.'

Tony frowned. 'And then what?'

'Then, I have a plan to destroy the 1066 club and execute their members. But we have to interrogate the prisoners first. I contacted the lads guarding them, and everything's fine. What I neglected to tell them is that we'll be arriving at two separate times in two different vans, just in case we get set up.'

'But why do we have to speak to the prisoners when we've got David Ryder? He would know the dates, wouldn't he?'

'Only the club members receive that information. The staff don't get told until the day before.'

The meeting concluded once they had finished their tea and coffee. With a few hours to spare, they spent quality time with their families. For Tony, it was a pleasant distraction from the serious issues he had to attend to, but the time went by far too quickly. It seemed like no time at all had passed before Bob was signalling to him with a wag of his finger. It tugged at his heart to leave his family behind again. He kissed and hugged Charlie and Doris and reserved a special, longer kiss for Veronica. He didn't want to let her go.

Bob shook his head. 'Can you two lovers let each other go? We've got work to do.'

'Love you all; see you soon,' Tony said as he let go of Veronica and followed Bob out of the room.

Tony wasn't the only one who looked like he didn't want to leave. Bob sighed as he looked around at them all. 'You don't want to go just yet – I get it – nor do I, but we've got to keep the impetus up and put as much pressure on our enemies as we can. I want that 1066 filth running scared.'

Bob led them out to the driveway. 'Tony, Harry, and Mickey – you're with me. The rest of you are in the other van. My team will leave first. Give us a fifteen-minute head start. Once we've reached the house and I'm sure it's safe, I'll text Richard. If you don't receive a text, do not enter the house. Is that clear?'

They nodded as they headed into their allocated vans. Tony sat in the front passenger seat exchanging small talk with Bob.

The journey to London was yet again boring and uneventful, but the constant babble of pop music made it pass a little easier. He watched the scenery along the way, tapping his fingers on the dashboard and enjoying moments of relaxation between the chatter.

When they arrived at their destination, they prepared for a shoot-out. They had no idea what awaited them but were ready for a worst case scenario in any case. Tony's heart pounded, but he felt as ready for this as he would ever be.

Bob hit the doorbell on the front door. Within a matter of a few seconds, a silhouette of a man appeared on the frosted glass window. The door opened, and one of the politicians' jailers, Martin Riley, gave them a welcoming smile. Tony relaxed as they were all invited in.

Bob stepped inside first, with Tony, Harry, and Micky following. 'How are our guests? Are they behaving themselves?'

'They're well taken care of.'

Martin led them down to the basement where they had been keeping the prisoners. Bob drew his weapon again, and the others followed suit. Martin's forehead frowned, and his eyes darted from side to side; they had no way of knowing if Martin was leading them into a trap or not.

As they entered the basement, Carl, the second guard, greeted them. Bob glanced around the basement, then rifled through his pockets. 'Best text the others to tell them that all's well,' he said and headed back up the stairs to get a signal. He returned a couple of minutes later.

With a nod from Bob, Carl unlocked the first cell door. Giles Campbell was sprawled on top of the bed, reading a book. He didn't bother looking up.

Bob turned to Martin, who was standing just outside the cell. 'There're four more from our team on the way.

Can you let them in for me when they arrive?'

'No problem, Bob. If you need anything, let Carl know.'

'Yeah, okay, Martin, thanks.'

Bob offered his hand to Campbell. 'Mr Campbell, it's so good to see you.'

Campbell's gaze flickered up from his book, but his expression remained cold.

Bob rubbed his hands together. 'Let's begin with the questions, shall we?' He gave Campbell an unusual, twisted smile. 'I'm going to ask you a series of questions, and you will answer them as accurately as possible. If your answers match up with the others we ask you, there will be no problems. However, if you fill me up with a load of bullshit, you'll regret lying to me.'

Campbell stared at Bob with deadpan eyes.

'We know where your family is, Mr Campbell. I don't need to spell out what that means, do I?'

'My family are guarded by the Security Services. I very much doubt your little… team… would gain access to them.'

'You're sure about that, are you? Our surveillance tells a different tale. No one's guarding your family. Whether you believe me or not, Mr Campbell, is your choice. Are you prepared to take that gamble?'

Carl stepped outside the room, and Bob slammed the door shut. Campbell shut his book. Tony stood in awe at how Bob went about his business. He knew Bob was bluffing, but he was damned good at it.

Campbell placed the book on the bedside table. 'What is it you want to know?'

'The date of the next human sacrifice.'

Campbell gasped, and his face drained of colour. He took a moment to answer, 'Easter Monday, at four o'clock.'

Bob smiled. He turned away from Campbell and addressed Harry, Micky, and Tony. 'Go into the other cells and ask them the same question.'

Footsteps echoed down the staircase as the second half of their team arrived. Tony said a quick hello, but there was no time to stop and chat. He entered the cell Carl had just opened for him and mimicked Bob's style. The threat of hurting the cellmate's family got him talking and confirming what Campbell had said.

Once everyone had finished questioning the prisoners, they reported their findings back to Bob. The prisoners had confirmed the same date and time.

'Let's get back to Kent,' Bob said. 'I'll have a good think about this and get something drawn up. Then we can discuss the best way forward. There will be no more human sacrifices, though. I'll make sure of that.'

The two groups of four departed from the holding centre in Neasden and drove back in a convoy to the farmhouse in Kent.

Easter Monday was only a week away. Whatever Bob was thinking had to be done fast, accurately, and had to be achievable. If they were successful, it would be the final mission. One wrong step and everything could end in disaster, and there would be nobody left to stop the 1066 group from destroying the nation.

SERFDOM AND DISORDER

28

The day after the trip to Neasden, Bob called another meeting. He waited for them all to settle down and then stood up at the head of the table, tall and imposing. 'I've had a look at a multitude of things since we got back, and my conclusion is this: The only way we can access the 1066 club is by going underground.'

There were mixed expressions around the table – open mouths, bemusement, cringing, and a few no's.

'Ah, I see you've concluded that we're going into the club via the sewers. But don't worry, lads' – he grinned – 'I'll make sure you're kitted out for the journey through the shit pit.'

Tony wondered how they were going to get into the club now David had stopped working there. 'How are we going to get in? There's no one working for us in the club anymore, is there?'

Bob grinned. 'Well, that's where you're wrong. We couldn't risk having only one man inside in case they caught on to what David was up to. Tom's been there for quite a while now, and he works in the upper part of the building. I won't bore you with how I met him, but he has the highest of clearances he could have as a staff member. I kept quiet about him to protect him, but after this business with you and David, all the rest of the staff got interrogated. It was tough for Tom, but he pulled through.'

Bob outlined how they would enter the club. 'Once we've gotten through the sewers and found the club's drain hole cover, there's a metal ladder that leads up to it. Tom will be waiting for us and let us in.'

John raised his head to speak. 'Will Tom guide us to a safe spot where we can hide until it's time to take action?'

'Yes, that's all covered. There's nothing to worry about there.'

Simon rubbed his hand on his stubble around his face. 'Do you plan to execute *all* the club's members and destroy the place?'

'That's the plan. There'll be a lot of people in attendance, which means there'll be private armed security and the Knights of Bayeux to contend with. It won't be a walk in the park, that's for sure.'

Harry sighed and shrugged his shoulders. 'What about our prisoners? What are we going to do with them? And what are we going to do with the prisoners who aren't club members?'

'If we have no further purpose for them and we defeat the 1066 group's plans, we can hand them over to the police that are not corrupted by our foes. John will sort that out.' Bob looked around the rest of the table. 'Any more questions?'

They all shook their head, seemingly content with Bob's plans. Tony was desperate to finish with the whole sorry saga. It had had a major impact on his life, a chapter he wanted to close.

Bob nodded. 'Okay, gents, I think with all the hard work we've put in, we can take a break for a few days. I want these premises vacated as of this afternoon. Everyone's to report back on Saturday morning. Oh, and make sure you're armed.'

His face took on a sombre expression as he put his hand inside his jeans pocket and pulled out a bag of pills. 'Cyanide pills. I know this sounds drastic and over-the-top, but we have to address this. We'll be leaving here for a few days. There's a possibility that one or more of us could get captured, and you know what that means. You'll get a pill each. There's no need to be worried. It's just a precaution. So don't go having sleepless nights over it, and whatever you do – don't lose it.'

Bob handed out the pills, which were sealed in a small plastic bag.

'One more thing,' Bob said. 'Don't go back to wherever you were living before this nonsense with the 1066 group is over.' He rapped on the table with a grin. 'Right, you lot, piss off. I don't want to see your ugly faces again until Saturday.'

29

The mission to attack the 1066 club was planned with expert precision. Differences of opinion surfaced and there was some intense discussion, but eventually, they agreed on a course of action.

They said an emotional farewell to their families. Tony just wanted it to be over. As the van pulled away from the farmyard, he lowered the window and leaned his head out for one last goodbye to Veronica, Doris, and Charlie, and then set himself to the task of psyching himself up for the battle ahead. To keep himself calm, he watched the countryside passing by; it helped ease his mind. He hated London, and having to go back there for violent confrontation made him hate the place even more.

Something felt different about this journey. It didn't take Tony long to work out what was missing. He glanced at Bob. 'What happened to the cheesy pop music you like listening to?'

'You're a cheeky bastard, ain't ya?' Bob said without taking his eyes off the traffic before him. He turned off the road they were on and headed up the slip road to the motorway. 'You love pop music just as much as I do. Just for you, Tony, I'll put the radio on.'

A classic pop song from the seventies blared out, lightening the atmosphere in the van. Tony grinned and tapped along to the music.

'Deep down,' Bob continued, 'I think you love these journeys down the motorway. You're like a kid going on a day trip. Am I right?'

Tony laughed. Bob's observation was one hundred percent correct.

'I'm right, ain't I? Don't worry. If it helps you cope with a mission, then it's worth it. You want to be in my mind if think you're bad. Why d'you think I always have pop music on the radio?'

'To help make the journey more relaxing and not so boring?'

'No. The sounds take me back to when I was younger and enjoying life in total naivety. It takes me on a nostalgia trip. So don't think its stupid drifting off to the past; its normal.'

Bob's words gave Tony some reassurance. He didn't feel like such a nostalgic fool anymore. 'So what sort of weapons are we taking on this trip?'

'You helped load the van up. Didn't you look at what we were putting inside?'

'They're in wooden crates. I didn't pack the cases, did I?'

'I told you at the meeting what we were taking. Weren't you listening? You weren't, were you? Thinking about Veronica, no doubt?'

Tony realised he had made himself look foolish again. 'You're right. I suppose it's the stress making my head lopsided.' Even as he said it, his mind went into overdrive.

The vans crossed the iconic Tower Bridge. Tony glanced at the River Thames flowing beneath them. In front of them, the City of London came into view. Its tall, glass, and steel office buildings contrasted with the Tower of London on their left, a structure that had been built by the 1066 group's ancestors, the Normans.

Tony stared at the Tower as they drove over the bridge. 'Do you think the 1066 group had anyone tortured or murdered in there?'

Bob laughed. 'It wouldn't surprise me. They've been going as a movement for centuries. Just think, if we fail today, we might even get sent there.'

Tony shook his head, and Bob laughed even more. To make matters worse, he turned up the volume on the radio and started singing.

They drove further into Bank, and the 1066 club drew nearer. Tony glanced at Bob as he parked the van on the curb. 'Bob, if I don't pull through this mission, I want you to give this to Veronica' – he handed Bob a passport-sized photo of himself and Veronica – 'and tell her how much I love her.'

Bob took the photo. 'I'll be giving this back to you on our journey home. Don't worry, we'll pull through this.' Bob offered him his hand. Tony shook it, acknowledging the symbol of unity and brotherhood.

'Don't stress yourself out. Once the ball gets rolling, you'll be fine.'

They exited the van casually. Just as they'd disembarked, the other van pulled up behind them. Bob raised his thumb to Richard, who drove the other van.

Richard returned the gesture, suggesting that everything was okay.

Their kit was in the rear of the van Tony had travelled in. Harry and Mickey had laid out everything out for them.

They placed red "road closed" and "men at work" signs near the stretch of road where they were going underground and changed into their protective outfits. The weaponry had been placed in waterproof packaging and stuffed inside large sports bags that each team member would carry.

They walked up to the large metal drainage cover in the centre of the road. Tony looked around without trying to seem suspicious; although, it was a bank holiday, Monday afternoon, so the street was empty – almost. A City of London policeman, with his distinct red-and-white chequered band across his navy cap, turned into the street and walked towards them. Tony tugged at Bob's sleeve. 'Fuck it,' he whispered. 'Don't look now, but there's a copper heading this way.'

'Is he on his own?'

Tony nodded.

Bob walked towards the van. He gave the policeman a quick glance and nodded. The policeman scowled back; he looked as stiff as a board. He approached Bob as he was about to undo the back of the van.

'You've shut the road down,' he said, gesturing to one of the road signs. 'I've had no information about this. What's going on?'

'We got a call about an hour ago. There's a blockage in the drainage system, and we've been sent here to clear it. We're the emergency crew. We go where we're sent and do as we're told. You know how it is.' His attempt at small talk didn't impress the officer. 'Right, I'll fetch the paperwork.'

The officer nodded. 'Good idea.'

Bob returned from the driver's side with a smile on his face and handed the paperwork over. The officer scrutinised it. His expression gave nothing away, then his gaze broke and he smiled as he handed the sheet of paper back. 'That all looks in order. I should have received a notification about this, though.'

'Sorry about that. I'll have a word with the office when I get back.'

The policeman smiled again and walked away. Everyone breathed a collective sigh of relief as he disappeared around the corner. Tony looked at Bob. 'That was lucky. If he'd been more persistent, we'd be in trouble now.'

'No. If anyone would have been in trouble, it was him.'

'What do you mean?'

Bob raised his eyebrows, and Tony realized what he meant. They couldn't risk getting arrested or tangling with an armed response unit.

Bob grabbed a couple of iron pins from the van and walked to the manhole. He passed one to John, and they slotted the metal pins into the grooves on the cover and lifted it out of its fixed position. Their faces turned red with the strain of carrying over to the curbside, where it landed with a metallic clang.

As Bob lowered himself into the manhole and down a set of steps, he turned to face those behind him. 'Right, lads, this is it. There's no going back now.'

SERFDOM AND DISORDER

One by one, each of them went down the hole in their full kit, complete with gas masks and their sports bags. Tony's stomach tightened as he descended into the dark, murky underworld where shit was king. It was a thirty-foot drop from the surface, and the closer he got to the bottom, the more lucid the view of turds floating around in water.

Tony reached the bottom and found himself standing in a stream just below knee height. He wanted to throw up and had to discipline himself from doing so.

Bob walked away from the pack, and they followed him like rats following the Pied Piper. He stopped a short distance away beside a metal ladder that escalated towards another man-hole cover. Everyone followed him up.

Tony was right behind Bob, struggling beneath the weight of the bag he carried. His lower back, upper arms, and thighs were aching, but he continued his upward climb without complaint.

Bob stopped at the top of the ladder, as did everyone behind him. He tapped the drain cover a few times. About a minute went by. The cover hadn't moved. Bob tapped again. Thirty seconds went by, and there was still no answer. Bob tapped again, this time the cover came off.

Tony feared the worst, convincing himself that they had run into difficulties and that it was the Knights of Bayeux opening the cover to them. None of them had easy access to their weapons. He held his breath as a light shone from the exposed manhole. The face of a man, who looked like he was in his early thirties, covered his nose with his hand as he leaned over the hole. Bob gave the thumbs up signal to Tony who did to the man below him, letting him know Tom had arrived. *What a fucking relief.*

Bob climbed out of the hole. Tony waited for Bob to show his face again and give him the all clear. He gripped the metal ladder as he glanced upward, hoping that Bob hadn't been nabbed.

A few moments passed before he saw Bob again, and then he climbed up, desperate to get out of the sewer. He emerged in a small room, about fifteen-by-fifteen feet. The white-tiled walls looked dirty, and the floor was grey concrete. It looked as if the room existed solely to allow workers access in and out of the sewer.

Tony took off his mask and stepped away from the drain hole, holding his hand over his nose. He watched as each member of the team rose out of the hole. Everyone looked relieved to get out of the sewers, though they all looked as sick as Tony felt.

Bob glanced around at them all. 'Okay, you're all here now. I want you to move fast. Get out of your outfits and into these overalls and training shoes.' He pointed to a pile of navy-blue overalls heaped on a seat. They were similar to the ones they'd used on the mission to the drugs warehouse in Poplar. Each pair of overalls had a nametag on them.

They changed out of their shit-stained outfits in rapid time, casting them aside. He called out to each member of the team and handed them their overalls and training shoes.

'How did you know our sizes?' Richard asked as he was pulled on his overalls and shoes.

'Bob, who else?'

SERFDOM AND DISORDER

Once they were dressed, they grabbed their bags, ready to move on.

Simon wrinkled his nose. 'What will happen to all those rubber suits?'

Bob smiled. 'Allow me to show you.'

Bob walked over to the broom propped up in the middle of the room, took a hold of it, and swept the suits down the manhole.

Bob threw the broom back against the wall and looked to Tom. 'Shall we go?' He glanced at his men. 'Get your handguns at the ready. You never know who we'll encounter in this place.'

Tom opened the door a little and peered outside, then stuck his head out and glanced around. Bob stood behind him, holding his Beretta 92 handgun to his chest, ready for action should the need arise.

Tony glanced at the rest of the team. He couldn't resist a witty remark before leaving the room. 'We look like a load of extras from a dystopian movie with these overalls on.'

There were a few sniggers and smiles. Bob rolled his eyes, but he was smirking too.

Tom turned around. He waved his arm, signalling that it was safe to move on. They followed him out of the room and along a narrow corridor with nothing either side of it but dreary, grey walls. They continued cautiously, as if something untoward might happen at any minute.

Tony's thoughts filled with war and revenge. He was eager to get started. *Let's hope I see that bastard – Mr Measurier – and make sure he remembers who I am.*

Tom stopped before an old door. It was painted

white but was filthy and had paint peeling off it. The door creaked as he opened it, putting the men more on edge than they were already. They all had their handguns drawn and pointed towards the door. Tom went through it first. After what seemed like an eternity, Tom returned, gesturing that all was well and that they could enter the main building with him.

There was a flight of wooden stairs on the other side that was wide enough to accommodate the men adequately. Tom went up first, ten steps ahead of them. Bob went next and the others followed behind, keeping their handguns drawn at the ready. They took the steps slowly to avoid making too much noise.

As Tom reached the top of the staircase, he froze and waved his hand for the rest of the team to move back. For a moment, Tony had no idea why and then he heard it –footsteps.

The team backed out of sight as the mystery person spoke to Tom. 'What are you doing in this part of the building? It's reserved for security personnel only.' The man sounded condescending.

'I… I had to speak to your chief of security. We received some news concerning a potential threat.'

The raid was over before it had begun. *The bastard's led us into a trap.* He clenched his teeth as he glared at Tom's back, tightening his grip on the handle of his Glock 30SF handgun.

Bob placed a hand on Tony's arm and raised his index finger to his lips, urging him to remain quiet and calm.

The conversation continued between Tom and what appeared to be a member of the internal security team.

'Look, I'm just following orders. I was told to pass the message onto your boss, if that's okay with you.'

'There's no one else in this part of the building. I was just doing a patrol, to see that everything was okay. I'll pass your message on. You can go back downstairs.'

'I'm not going until I see your boss. I know he's up here.'

'Look, buddy boy, if you don't go back downstairs in the next ten seconds, I'll shoot you dead.'

It didn't sound like the man was going to budge. Bob winked at Tony then crept quietly up the stairs, his arms expanded with the pistol pointing ahead of him. He sprinted up the last few stairs, stopped to aim, and fired. With his silencer fitted, the shots emitted only a dull sound; the body tumbling down the stairs made more noise. The corpse stopped by Tony's feet, his dead eyes staring straight at him. The man had been in his thirties and was wearing a full khaki uniform. Tony wanted to kick the corpse, such was the hatred he felt.

Bob came down the stairs, unfazed by what had just happened. He crouched beside the corpse and then tossed the dead body over his shoulder. 'Come on, let's dump this wanker upstairs somewhere and then we can go from there.'

Tom carried on leading the way. They arrived at another door, and he opened it with caution, glanced outside, then gave the all clear.

The team was escorted to a huge balcony overlooking a hall. Bob dumped the corpse in a corner as if it were nothing more than garbage and returned to the rest of the team.

They crouched behind the four-foot high railings.

The hall was empty for now and in darkness. Tom looked around at the team. 'I'll make up some excuse for our friend over there,' he said, nodding towards the corpse. 'Let's hope the security chief doesn't smell anything suspicious. The ceremony won't start for another hour, so it's best to lay low until then. Good luck, everybody.'

The team all shook hands with Tom and thanked him as he departed the balcony area. He had to continue in his role as an employee of the 1066 club for now and couldn't afford to be caught anywhere near the hall.

Bob whispered as the group gathered close. 'Right, let's get our hardware out of the bags and ready ourselves for what's in store. We've come this far; this is only just the beginning.'

30

The waiting game was over. The lights in the main hall turned on, and the interior came to life. Medieval banners of differing designs hung on the walls, and there were marquees with red, white, and blue stripes scattered around. The exposed parts of the walls not covered with Norman memorabilia looked like that from an Old English castle. It looked authentic, like a film studio that was making a movie set in the Norman period. Dangling from the ceiling hung baskets of flowers in a variety of colours.

Tony gawked, entranced by what he saw. As his focus drifted to the stage area, his eyes widened. There were five wooden stakes, about eight feet high, rising out of the stage, and attached to the stakes were thick chains.

Harry glanced at Tony. 'That's where the human sacrifices are performed. They chain the victims to the stakes and then...' Harry moved his index finger across his throat.

Staff members came and went, adding the finishing touches to the event, including tankards of ale to the marquees. Armed guards took position around various parts of the hall. It looked both beautiful and menacing. From out of the blue, medieval music flowed from wall-mounted speakers – flutes, harps, lutes, and drums added legitimacy to the event.

Tony sat with his back against the balcony wall, as did the others, reflecting on the beauty of the music. *It's like going back to the twelfth century.* Tony couldn't resist a peek over the balcony again.

The guests were beginning to arrive. All the men entering were dressed as Norman noblemen, in an outer-flowing cloak, and an inner all-in-one tunic that fell below their knees. The colours they had dressed in varied.

They entered various marquees, as if each member had been designated a certain place. Once they were in place, a hoard of women entered the hall. They were dressed in period costume, their heads coved with a scarf, a flowing cloak, and an inner all-in-one tunic that trailed to the floor. The material seemed softer, shinier, and more colourful.

The women entered the marquees, and it wasn't long before the volume increased. Laughter and the sound of smacked flesh brought down the veneer of respectability as the sexual fun and games began. Groans and orgasmic screams accompanied the music, and tankards of ale was freely available. The whole thing sounded debauched and perverted, but that was the reason the prostitutes had been brought in.

The team returned to sitting with their backs against the balcony's wall. It wasn't easy to sit and listen to the orgy going on just below them. Tony glanced at a few of his brothers in arms. From the look on their faces they seemed about ready to jump over the balcony and join in the orgy.

Mickey smiled. 'Fuck, I wished I had a Norman outfit. Listen to them; they're fucking each other senseless. I could handle one of those prostitutes while drinking wine from a silver goblet.'

Simon leaned towards Mickey. 'Who would you be if you dressed up, William the Conqueror?'

'I don't know about me. Those blokes are doing all of the conquering at the moment.'

Everyone laughed. Tony, however, was thinking about Veronica and what he wanted to do with her if he managed to pull through the mission. In his mind's eye, he imagined himself and Veronica dressed in Norman period clothing and having sex on a large four-poster bed.

The drinking and sex continued for another two hours. A few of the team looked edgy and agitated as they waited for the mission to get moving. But then a loud fanfare of trumpets blasted around the hall. Tony peeked a look over the balcony. There were ten trumpeters dressed in traditional outfit on the stage. Their fanfare was, it seemed, a signal to end the frolics.

The prostitutes were hurried from the hall with no time to dress. They held their clothes in a bundle across their chests and ran together in a long line towards the exit door. A further ten minutes passed where nothing happened. It seemed this was to give the men time to get dressed and prepare for what was to come next.

The marquees rose upward to the ceiling via an electronic device with ropes attached to it, enabling the marquees to leave the hall at speed.

Another regal fanfare of trumpets began, but this time shouting and screaming accompanied it. Tony and Bob poked their heads over the balcony to see where the noise had come from. The hall had divided in two. On one side were the members dressed as Norman nobility. On the other were what Tony assumed to be the Knights of Bayeux, dressed in full Norman battle outfits: metal mesh tunics, pointed metal helmets with a strip that covered the nose, together with swords and shields. The scene looked organised and structured.

After the fanfare, there was total silence. A man in his sixties, sporting a grey beard and a pot belly and dressed as Norman nobility, walked up the side staircase that led up to the stage and stood to the side.

Then came the victims, both men and women, for the sacrifice. They were led onto the stage looking both confused and scared. They wore sack-like garments without sleeves that went down to their knees. Some of the prisoners were shaking and seemed uncertain about their fate.

A tall, bulky man in a black mask that covered the whole of his head, with the exception of his eyes, nose, and mouth, chained each of the victims to a stake. He sneered and growled at the prisoners as he tied them up. The sacrifices tried to put up a struggle, but it was a useless gesture. They screamed to be let free, but their cries were met with cold indifference. The executioner shoved a gag over their mouths, and their eyes bulged with terror.

The nobleman walked to the forefront of the stage as another fanfare of trumpets greeted him. 'Welcome

SERFDOM AND DISORDER

to all of you standing before me. I send you my gratitude. I also pledge gratitude for our Norman ancestors – blood brothers and all. Within the total time spent on this earth, we shall remain together as brothers no matter what.

'Tonight is a special night, for we have new members entering the fold and we also observe this calendar day with reverence. To all gathered here tonight, are we unified? Are we proud of our heritage and our ancestors?'

The man waited for a response from the audience with his chest puffed outward in arrogance.

'Aye, that we are,' the men replied in unison.

'To celebrate our unity and welcome new members into our group, we offer these people as a sacrifice to the gods and to reinforce our authority on British society. Long may it reign.'

Again, the bearded man stood silent, waiting for a response.

'Long may it reign,' the men in the hall replied.

The speech and unified responses sounded remote, nasty, and unsympathetic. It made the fate awaiting the sacrificial victims seem much worse. Until now, they had been unaware of their fate. The prisoners attempted to scream but were subdued by the gags. They struggled against their bonds and tears streamed down their faces. They understood their time was coming to a close.

The man in black approached the first victim. He withdrew a gleaming, long sword from a leather sheath and raised it above his head.

Bob pulled out a grenade, flicked off the pin, and tossed it into the crowd before repeating the manoeuvre. Explosions went off, shaking the hall. Shouts of horror reverberated around.

The executioner spun around to face the crowd. As he did, Harry fired a single shot from his L11SA3 sniper rifle. The executioner's head exploded on impact. His sword and torso fell to the floor, and the hall descended into chaos. Shots were fired towards the balcony, and club members attempted to run from the fires caused by the grenades. Bodies were strewn across the floor, and there were screams of agony. Some members had missing limbs and were covered in blood.

Before anyone could escape from the hall, Micky tossed grenades over the balcony and more explosions erupted, together with more bloodied cries of anguish and pain. Every member of the team had their sniper rifles cocked over the edge of the balcony, and they picked off those below. Butterflies erupted in Tony's stomach as he focused on who to kill next.

Mayhem erupted in the hall, and Tony flinched as bullets zipped past him.

Mickey winked at Tony and grinned. 'Hold it together. This is not the time to lose your bottle.' He tossed some grenades over the balcony. Booms echoed as the building shook.

Bob crawled along the floor towards Tony and Mickey and shouted over the din. 'I think some of the knights of Bayeux are hiding at the side of the stage area. We can't lob grenades near there. Those poor bastards chained to the stakes will cop it too. We need to get nearer.'

Tony's eyes widened as he wiped the sweat off his brow. He stared at Bob, uncertain of what he had in store for those below. Shots continued to ring out from the hall.

How the fuck are they managing to fire shots back? They should be dead and gone by now.

Bob pulled out the Carl Gustav anti-tank rocket launcher from his bag and lifted it onto his shoulder. 'Cover me.'

The men let off a rally of firepower towards the hall and the side of the stage. The helpless fuckers chained to the stake flinched as bullets whistled past them.

Bob took aim and fired into the middle section of the hall. There was a massive boom on impact. Smoke billowed everywhere, and a huge crater appeared in the floor, exposing the level below.

Each member of the team pulled a rope and grappling hook out of from their sports bag at a frantic pace. They opened the hook and threw them upward, hoping it would connect on the metal-framed ceiling. Like a well-mechanised machine, they connected the ropes without trouble.

Tony's heart pounded as he realised it was time to slide into the blood-soaked, blitzed hall. He watched as each of his teammates slid down, with their rifles strapped onto their shoulders, firing off rounds from their PP-2000 sub-machine guns as they did so. Bob not only had a rifle strapped around his left shoulder, but he also carried the rocket launcher on his right shoulder. Tony wondered how he did it.

Oh, well, here I go.

He jumped outward, caught the rope, and slid down at speed, giving his hands a mild burning sensation. He would have loved to have slid down it firing his gun, but sadly, he wasn't experienced enough for that.

At ground level, the carnage and destruction looked even worse. There were men with lumps of flesh torn away from them; massive amounts of blood splattered everywhere. He heard cries of anguish, and still the Knights of Bayeux fought back.

Tony let off a rally of shots towards the stage as he dived to the ground for cover and slid in a pool of blood.

Bob signaled for Tony, Mickey and Harry to go to the side of the stage on the left, whilst signaling to the others to go to the right.

Tony followed Mickey, Bob and Harry. Somebody fired from the side of the stage, killing one of the chained prisoners. The other prisoners' faces became ghostly white. Tony could hear their muffled screams through the gags on their mouths.

Bob shouted. 'Come on lads, let's finish these fuckers off.'

Each man shouted as they charged forwards and lobbed their grenades to the side of the stage. Intense groaning sounded as the team darted to their designated destination. The Knights of Bayeux continued to battle from both the left and right.

Bob turned to Tony. 'Keep an eye on the people chained up, make sure they're safe.'

Tony nodded as the rest of the team rallied forward. More gunfire sounded, and some of the knights shouted out to surrender.

A shot rang out behind him, grazing Tony's upper left arm. From nowhere, a shadowy figure approached the stage and fired off shots. Rage engulfed Tony, and he let his automatic weapon do its job and finished off the shadowy figure.

Tony's colleagues appeared on the stage. Bob glanced at Tony then jumped down to inspect his arm. 'It's Ok Tony, just a nick, you'll live.'

Tony stared into Bob's eyes. 'I fucking hope so, mate.'

Bob laughed. 'Come on war hero, let's see if any of those blue blood bastards are still alive.'

It was brutal and harsh, but essential. Within a matter of minutes, the enemy all lay dead on the floor. Each member of the team continued to walk around the hall for any signs of life.

As Tony walked around the hall, stepping over dead bodies and bits of flesh and limbs, he noticed one of the bloodied men moaning and crying for help. It was the man from the club who made his life a misery – Mr Measurier.

Tony scowled. 'Remember me, you gin-soaked bastard?'

Measurier squinted as if trying to remind himself who stood before him. He smiled weakly, and in a strained, diluted voice said, 'Ah, yes, the boy who served me gin. You're here to save me?' Measurier raised his arm towards Tony.

Tony pressed the rifle to Measurier's forehead. 'Come to save you? You're all politeness now, ain't ya?'

Measurier's eyes widened, and he shook his head. 'Help me. I'll do anything you want.'

'Fuck you, you pompous, perverted, old fool. You'll get no sympathy from me!'

Tony fired into Measurier's forehead without remorse. He'd rid the world of someone who wasn't worthy of living on it.

It was a gory sight walking around the hall. Blood dripped off Tony's training shoes. Every now and then, a shot would be fired as another half-conscious club member or anyone who wasn't on the side of the good was executed.

There was little resistance from the 1066 group; the attack had been swift, and the Knights of Bayeux were no more. Everything was over.

Bob walked up to Tony. 'Come on, help me free those poor fuckers chained up. Don't worry about that arm, it's fuck all.'

They stepped over numerous bloodied bodies on their way, their shoes squelching as they walked to the side stairs that led up to the stage. The bound and gagged prisoners watched them with wide eyes and screamed behind their gags, struggling to free themselves.

'It's okay,' Bob said. 'There's no need to panic. We're the good guys. We're here to save you.'

The horrified looks melted. Tony and Bob removed their gags, and they cried tears of relief and gratitude.

'Tony, search that fucker for a set of keys,' he said, nodding towards the executioner, who once had a head. 'If he hasn't got them, check the other piece of shit, the one who gave the speech.'

Tony couldn't bring himself to look at the headless part of the executioner's body – the sight would have made him vomit – as he rifled through his clothes. He found the keys around the executioner's neck on a chain. Tony grimaced and tossed the keys to Bob.

Tony and Bob smiled at each other as the prisoners were unshackled from the stakes. He stared at the male prisoner who had been shot and became a little sad. He let out a sigh. *Sorry old mate, we couldn't save you.*

Bob patted Tony on the back. 'Unfortunately Tony there are always victims in wars. This is one of them. Focus on what we've achieved. We've saved our country mate. You should feel proud.'

It felt good to liberate the prisoners, and Tony experienced a huge swell of pride at reaffirming his humanity, having helped to save them from a grisly fate. The women hugged and kissed them, while the men shook their hands in gratitude and hugged them.

Tony looked around the once-grand hall. The stench of burnt flesh filled his nose. The menace to society had been eradicated, and he had held his own with the SAS boys.

He smiled. *I've served my country well.*

Tom escorted the team and the prisoners through a side door concealed to look like part of the decor, which lead them onto a street close to where the vans were parked.

Everybody, apart from Tom, loaded into the vans and headed back to Kent. Both vehicles drove away. Tony breathed a massive sigh of relief as he looked at Bob and smiled.

Bob turned on the radio. He grinned at Tony. 'Here's that photo of you and Veronica. I told you I'd be giving it back, didn't I?'

Tony's own smile grew as he took the photo from Bob, kissed it, and placed it inside his trouser pocket.

'There's just one thing to do to make all this complete now.'

'Yeah, what's that?'

'The crap radio station that churns out the pop music from the sixties, seventies, and eighties.'

Bob laughed. 'What do you think I turned it on for? Stop pretending its crap; you love it. Tonight, we'll be having a serious party.'

'Yeah, that sounds good.'

As Tony tapped his fingers in time to the music, the flashing lights appeared before his eyes, again, but with far more intensity. In an instant, he was no longer in the van but floating through a tunnel of light. Images seared through his mind – memories of another time and place.

The floating ended abruptly. He blinked to clear his vision and found himself lying on a bed with wires attached to his head. The room was bright white, but there were no walls. He was surrounded by a visible electrical force. He could hear the gentle hum of power. He squeezed his eyes shut and opened them again. Nothing changed. He sat up as his heart thudded and sweat trickled down his brow. *I have – I've gone mad!*

SERFDOM AND DISORDER

31

Tony forced himself to breathe and calm the fuck down. He was having a moment; that was all. He just needed to visualize the van, Bob, Veronica – the corny pop music – and he'd go back to where he was supposed to be. It was stress caused by the mission, that was all, but he couldn't shake off the feeling of not being himself – quite literally – the memories in his mind belonged to another man.

The hum of electricity lowered and then stilled. The electrical force around him faded, and two oddly dressed men stood before him, smiling.

'It's you,' Tony said, pointing a finger at the man in the black jumpsuit. 'Where the hell am I? What have you done to me?'

'Welcome home, Joel.' The second man said. 'There's nothing to alarm yourself about. It's natural to experience a little disorientation.'

Tony recognized the voice from the fleeting moments he had spent in the illusory tunnel. 'Joel?'

He shook his head and scrubbed his face with his hands. This was a dream. A *bad* dream or a psychotic episode, perhaps? That would explain a lot.

'Look at the sign, Joel,' the man in the jumpsuit said, pointing to a white-lettered sign on a black background which read: 'Holographic Department of Oxford University.'

'What the—'

'It's okay, you're perfectly safe, and there is no need to worry. My name is William Thompson, and this is Marcus Smith, who you will no doubt recognize, given time. You've been on quite an adventure.'

Marcus smiled. 'You're a history student, Joel. Tony Harrison was an important historical figure in the twenty-first century. His role in the demise of the 1066 group prevented Britain from becoming a tyrannical society. He followed in his Uncle Charlie's footsteps in studying and become a great lawyer, highly respected and very influential. Thanks to his insight, it wasn't just Britain that became a fairer, more inclusive society, but his work had a domino effect around the world.'

'He did?'

Memories of another life flashed through his mind in sharp bursts.

'We have a massive amount of history programmed into the holographic regenerator. All of our history students have the opportunity to visit whatever period in history they're studying, usually as a distant observer.'

'I'm afraid there was a glitch when you went in,' William explained. 'For reasons we have yet to fathom, you took on the identity of Tony Harrison. Everything that happened in there, every emotion, every fear, were real to you. Marcus and I have been working around the clock to try and free you from the program.'

SERFDOM AND DISORDER

'The tunnel of light…'

'You were so deeply ingrained in your desire to protect Veronica and destroy the 1066 group that we had to let the program run its course. The risk of causing irrevocable brain damage was just too high.'

'I loved her so much. I was going to marry her…'

William put a hand on Joel's shoulder. 'If it's any consolation, they shared a long and happy marriage and produced three children.'

Tony – no, he had to think of himself as Joel now – was relieved to know Tony and Veronica had stayed together, but he felt empty at the thought of never seeing her again. She was everything he loved in a woman. He grimaced as he reflected on all his friends, family, and team – they were nothing more than a computer program.

Marcus stepped forward. 'Your fiancée and family are waiting for you in the observation room. Now, sit still while I burst this bolt of energy in your ear.' He held up an oblong metallic device with lights flashing around it. 'There's no need to worry, Joel. This will rejuvenate your brain and help bring back the real you.'

A warm pulse of energy flowed through his brain, pleasant and uplifting. He relaxed and felt more alive. His face loosened.

He administered the burst and within a few minutes, Joel was escorted to a room where his fiancée and family sat waiting. They had all been in a state of high anxiety; although, what had been weeks for him had been only a few days to them.

Joel felt more like himself as he approached a glass door. It opened automatically, and as he stepped inside, he came face to face with his family and fiancée, Patricia. Everyone leapt from their seats in unison. They hugged and kissed him, and they all cried.

Patricia approached Joel with her arms outstretched. He froze. Patricia was Veronica's double, apart from her hairstyle, clothes, and make-up – and the gap of a few hundred years.

'Are you okay, Joel? You look like you've seen a ghost.'

'I'm perfect,' he said and pulled her body close to his and held her tightly. 'I – Tony – had a lover in the hologram. Veronica Jones. She was identical to you.'

'Well, she would be. She was an ancestor of mine on my mother's side. She helped Tony Harrison change the world, you know? It's because of her that you chose to focus on him for your Ph.D, seeing as he was directly involved in bringing down the 1066 group.'

Joel nodded. It was all coming back to him now. 'This is just too weird to take on board.' He was both dumbfounded and ecstatic. He kissed Patricia on her sweet lips with even more passion than before. The family left the room to give them some privacy.

Joel and Patricia left the room holding hands and smiling. Awaiting them, a crowd of university friends cheered Joel for getting through his ordeal. He had experienced something no one else had. His face flushed with all the attention.

His perceptions of life had changed; he became a more positive, reflective person, and he had Tony, Veronica, Bob, and the holographic computer program to thank for that.

I still feel as if Tony Harrison's inside me. I'll make sure his spirit lives on.

ABOUT THE AUTHOR

J P Gadston studied English literature at the University of East London, as a mature student.

He grew up in the east end of London and experienced the culture and the mindset firsthand. He now lives in the cosy Thames Estuary town of Leigh-on-Sea.

Gadston spends his time doing yoga, running, wing chun, chi-kung and meditating. He is a big advocate of personal development. No matter how bad it gets you keep on moving forward.

Gadston also enjoys travelling, particularly to Scandinavian countries. A lot of his time is spent reflecting on life and the bigger picture. He also is a big fan of music taking in most genres.

For more information about J P Gadston, please visit our website:

MIND UTOPIA PRESS

http://jp-gadston.co.uk/